THE LIQUOR VICAR

— — —

THE MILDLY CATASTROPHIC
MISADVENTURES OF TONY VICAR

— — —

The Liquor Vicar

Coming 2022:
The Vicar's Knickers

VINCE R.
DITRICH

THE
LIQUOR
VICAR

**THE MILDLY
CATASTROPHIC
MISADVENTURES
OF TONY VICAR**

DUNDURN
PRESS

Publisher and acquiring editor: Scott Fraser | Editor: Shannon Whibbs
Cover designer: Laura Boyle
Cover image: Illustration by Laura Boyle; car: adapted by Sophie Paas-Lang from shutterstock.com/Dmitry Natashin
Printer: Marquis Book Printing Inc.

Library and Archives Canada Cataloguing in Publication

Title: The liquor Vicar / Vince R. Ditrich.
Names: Ditrich, Vince R., 1963- author.
Identifiers: Canadiana (print) 20200376896 | Canadiana (ebook) 20200376950 | ISBN 9781459747258 (softcover) | ISBN 9781459747265 (PDF) | ISBN 9781459747272 (EPUB)
Classification: LCC PS8607.I87 L57 2021 | DDC C813/.6—dc23

We acknowledge the support of the Canada Council for the Arts and the Ontario Arts Council for our publishing program. We also acknowledge the financial support of the Government of Ontario, through the Ontario Book Publishing Tax Credit and Ontario Creates, and the Government of Canada.

Care has been taken to trace the ownership of copyright material used in this book. The author and the publisher welcome any information enabling them to rectify any references or credits in subsequent editions.

The publisher is not responsible for websites or their content unless they are owned by the publisher.

Printed and bound in Canada.

Dundurn Press
1382 Queen Street East
Toronto, Ontario, Canada M4L 1C9
dundurn.com, @dundurnpress

Dedicated to
Masters Oliver Vince & Parker Robert Alexander
Ditrich
Duo faciunt orbis terrarum

Prologue / Aqua Velveeta

She can't move. She is taped to a kitchen chair and wonders when her end will come. Listening carefully to the bizarre byplay of her kidnappers, she struggles to understand. The tall, dangerous beauty pacing around her is the unchallenged leader, narcissistic and steeped in a world visible only to herself. Her aims are achieved by alternating between graphic sexuality and brutal sadism. She is reckless, dangerous, volatile, and totally in control.

The minions surrounding her are incapable of anything other than obedience, lest they make their queen bee unhappy. None of them seems strong enough to put up any kind of resistance. The whole scenario is hard to believe, yet here it is, laid out.

What kind of tortured childhood did this kidnapper suffer? She screams for "the Vicar" once again, then spins dramatically on her heel. After casting about the place, she picks up the little cheddar slicer and brandishes it like a terrorist on a TV show. The victim imprisoned on the chair takes the threat seriously, yet also appreciates the absurd possibility that she will be killed courtesy of a shiv with the word *fromage* punched into its blade, which is being waved around wildly by a child in the body of a goddess. It is like some kind of morphine dream, a jumbled and scrambled Greek tragedy — but Oedipus didn't use a cheese knife.

The kidnapper moves back to the wall and screams something about doing a swap for the Vicar. Immobilized on the cracked vinyl, the hostage is frightened and powerless. At that moment, she senses Vicar's presence like a low-frequency thrum running through her chest. She can smell him, his aftershave. Something is afoot. She knows it.

One / Elvis Has Definitely Left the Building

Tony Vicar was jammed in a corner, but at least he was right beside the bar. It was a mobile affair on casters offering only battery-acid wine from a bag and urine-like beer in cans. Another damn wedding. He loathed them. The cheap rotgut would have to do.

A couple standing off to the side halfway along the room kept glancing up at his DJ booth. Only she spoke, while he nodded in wordless agreement. Clearly, she was informing him of what he thought. *A damned meat puppet*, thought Vicar.

He selected another track, cross-faded, and watched as a portly bridesmaid was asked to dance by some old fart pretending to be genteel. He wore generic black pants — pleated, with massive cuffs — old-man dress shoes — cushioned, practical, and hideous — and a coat with the nap of an indoor/outdoor mat, too tight to button up, though the wretched artifact had probably fit him a thousand Meat Lover's pizzas ago. Vicar imagined the cocktail napkin likely to be found in the left-hand pocket: square, blue, with silver print reading *Rotary Club Win and Dine '91*. It would be crumpled and have snot and a smear of late-twentieth-century brie on it. That jacket should come with a sermon.

Bridesmaid dresses were in abundance, the garb of self-flagellating public shame willingly borne by the girlfriends so as to lower public expectations of the bride — an uggo, otherwise why have her wedding at the world's oldest Eagles Hall, and why to that big meathead?

This bridesmaid, though. Behind a corsage as large as a Mesozoic rhododendron, her features were barely visible. She was cinched up in light-apricot and grey velveteen, a dress so alarmingly tight that the fair maiden in question looked like a knackwurst seconds from splitting on the barbie. Her gunt was going to blow clean through and engulf that old man who was sheathed in the tweed George Mallory died in. Vicar thought of the theatre scene from *The Blob*. Shit like this could drive a man to drink.

He shuddered, and without even looking, reached to his right, toward the long lineup of drinks he'd preordered, each to be downed in one greedy gulp. It helped, even though it tasted like unfiltered donkey piss. Just then, he saw the Meat Puppeteer prod her dutiful errand boy.

Skinny and hunched, as if revealing his whip marks to the entire gathering, he nervously shuffled toward the DJ booth. Vicar's eyes narrowed. It would be either "Take It Easy" or "Brown Eyed Girl." The bowed lackey glanced back at the Puppeteer for reassurance as he neared the podium, so Vicar knew it was "Brown Eyed Girl." That moron.

"Excuse me, we have a request. Do you take requests?"

Har-dee-fuckin'-har. "We" have a request. Vicar suppressed a smirk. *Do I take requests? No, no, I'm here for ART's sake, you stupid idiot.* Flatly, Vicar replied, "'Brown Eyed Girl'?"

The man's eyes opened wide. "How did you know?" he blurted.

Vicar lowered his voice so that it couldn't quite be heard over the current song. "The musically retarded always ask for that one first." *Second is "Old Time Rock and Roll," you thick fuck,* he added to himself. Hunched Meat Puppet couldn't make him out. He just offered an ingratiating smile and beat a retreat to his taskmistress.

Dark and getting darker by the minute, Vicar banged back two fast beers, squeezing the cans dramatically as if for show, although no one gave him a glance. He belched sonorously after finishing each one. He was nicely tipsy now and feeling entertained by the tableau before him. The best man approached and yelled in his ear: "They're going to do the first dance now. You have the song ready?"

Dismissively, Vicar said, "Yeah, yeah. Right here. Just gimme the sign."

The best man pulled out a script from his inside pocket and nervously looked it over. "Okay, I'll just give you a thumbs-up, like this." He eagerly demonstrated his cheery thumbs-up.

"A-okay, Buzz," Vicar responded dryly. Nonplussed, the best man smiled weakly and quickly departed.

With that, Vicar tried some of the wine in a bag. A headache in a sack. Hurl waiting to be hurled. Pish in, puke out. Blush hemlock Chablis. Hopefully, an atrocity strong enough to kill him before some stupid cowpoke's mother-in-law requested the "Bird Dance."

There was some kind of commotion, and people started gathering and shuffling around, clearly in preparation for this, the last stupid fucking item on the list of stupid fucking things done by people with beige and white houses in the stupid fucking suburbs who'd never had an original thought in their stupid fucking lives. If, heaven forbid, the roof ever collapsed on the local Costco, they'd all perish simultaneously, crushed into a slurry of factory-made salsa and discontiguous body parts.

He mumbled now, edgy and resentful, nicely pissed, and richly enjoying his saturated, boozy perception in the disco lights. It was a welcome distraction from his worsening mood. How in the hell had he gotten *here*? He had been denied by the fates. He had practised it, he had imagined it, he had lived it. But he'd never quite been able to loft himself over the top. He had dreamed of being big time, yet here he was, barely employed, in the dim corner of this decrepit banquet room.

Best Man gave the thumbs-up, and Vicar faded into the pre-selected song. He dutifully made an announcement — he didn't even slur much — then played the song.

He watched the groom — probably only his second time in a suit — clumsily steer his tittering bride around the floor. *Good Christ, she's wearing a headband. Ha! Get her some wristbands, too.* Vicar immediately dubbed her Chunderwoman. As the wedding party circled around and took photos, he got on the microphone and began to sing along with Anne Murray in mock exultation. "Do I get this *dunce* for the rest of my life?" A few people noticed and grimaced, but he just cackled and downed another beer.

For emergencies he had a bottle of Johnnie Walker Red in his case. It was an emergency. He grabbed a wineglass and ice and filled it with his smuggled Scotch hidden under the linen tablecloth, then camouflaged himself behind a centrepiece so ghastly and obese that he'd left it there for laughs and worked it into the show. Cheap carnations and funeral-home lilies. He muttered to himself, "Very interesting ... but schtoopid." His silly pantomime was such an ancient comedy reference that no one even smiled as he leered through the flower stalks.

He grimly downed the four-ounce serving of Scotch on the rocks and felt a bracing burn. Setting aside the glass and taking a breath, he gathered up his costume and began putting it on. He had been reduced to this: a DJ who did an Elvis impersonation.

Oh, how the excitement built as people began to take notice of his costume. A white, bedazzled Superman suit, spandex and magnificent. A full wig with adhesive sideboards. The classic Elvisian shades. A belt so baroque it made Batman's seem delicate. As Vicar stood up from his boot-donning crouch, he heard a gale of shrieks erupt. He looked around with disgust. *Don't tell me these idiots are going to be INTO this*, he thought. *Let's just get it over with so I can pocket the extra hundred bucks, and they can get back to their curling bonspiels.*

■ ■ ■

The mood shifts as the lights change to red and blue. Tony Vicar drunkenly cues up the playlist of his Elvis medley and starts the audio, which commences with the low, sustained notes of "Also Sprach Zarathustra" — theme of 2001: A Space Odyssey *and epic Elvis walk-on number. The crowd surges toward him, and he has a long haul on yet another Scotch. Ronnie Tutt's double kick drum intro starts up, and Elvis Vicar enters the building.*

He starts flailing his hips, and some of the older women look up apprehensively as Vicar concludes that they haven't witnessed a gyrating crotch in years. Everyone is grinning. His gut is barely contained by the spandex. Elvis launches energetically into "See See Rider." The crowd is jumping up and down. One woman clad in dusty-rose chiffon ululates excitedly but is unable to clap in time, not even on one and three. She is so haphazard that she nearly forces Vicar off the groove. He wonders if she is hearing impaired and turns away.

He is drunk, already out of breath before the first chorus and putting serious welly into something he detests doing. With blazing-fast tempo into a dramatic stop, Ronnie Tutt gives two Bucket of Fish drum fills and then, boom, right into the next tune, "An American Trilogy." During the big pause before "Glory, Glory, Hallelujah," Vicar takes another huge pull on the Scotch. At the climactic lyric, "His truth is marching on," he feels a clench of peristalsis in his lower bowel on the high note and hopes he hasn't just shat his white costume.

He is fully, obviously intoxicated now, stumbling, slurring. He loses his footing on the step and cracks his arm down on the DJ rig. It glitches and starts playing "The Wreck of the

Edmund Fitzgerald." Too drunk to fix the problem, he just starts Elvising out Lightfoot lyrics as they flash through his muzzy mind. Guttural lines like "Hey fellas, yeahhh, it's too rough to feed ya … in the ghetto."

Someone cracks up laughing at that, so he makes it a theme. "You ain't nothin' but a big lake they call Gitche Gumee … in the ghetto." His head lolls randomly as he delivers the low notes. With no concept of how far off centre his bubble is, he thinks he's pulling it off with aplomb.

The pretty bartender, her eyes crinkled possibly in amusement, has had her jaw agape for at least three entire minutes, licking her lips anxiously as though she can't quite comprehend the vision before her.

Elvis begins his requisite but ill-conceived Kingly karate moves, teetering dangerously, kicking wildly, yipping "hi-yah" bizarrely, and finally finding it impossible to get back up from his dramatic ducking manoeuvre. He is stuck on his haunches, lowing, "In the ghetto … and his mamma cried," like a forlorn yak stuck in a creek bed. Through the fog it dawns on him that he may have touched cloth during his perilous squat. By now the room has begun to turn on the King. The older, more sober folks are departing, most of them hastening to the coat check.

The music fades out to silence, and he is crouched in the wash of coloured light, wobbling precariously, slurring a great deal, and desperately needing a good crap. In a flash of inspiration, he announces in his best Elvis voice, "C'mon, ev'rabody. Come watch how the King met his end." Listing like the SS Andrea Doria and wilting to the floor, he shakily dismounts the stage, a small coterie of curious onlookers in tow. Sounding a lot more like Foghorn Leghorn than Elvis, he expounds, "I shall, I say, I shall re-create the last moments of Elvis Presley, the King of Rock and Roll. Yes, I, I, I shall show the world how we lost our King." As he marches directly toward the bathroom, he points at a boy of perhaps ten or eleven and foghorns, "Nice kid, but a little hmmm." The boy's mother draws him up in a protective embrace and looks back at Elvis with shock.

Upon entering the john, Elvis gets off his spandex pants, perches on the toilet with the stall door open, and begins singing vaguely about "bigga bigga hunks" of something or other. Apparently they'd doo, they'd doo. With that, his bowels unleash an acrid spray of hot liquid, and one of the women who has drunkenly followed him lets loose a blood-curdling scream, triggering the spectators to recoil in a whiplash of abject revulsion and bringing that portion of the evening's entertainment, and any future Tony Vicar might have had as an Elvis-impersonating wedding DJ, to a screeching halt.

Two / Jackie O with a Q

Vicar woke with a jarring splash of acid in his gut and realized he was badly hungover in a strange bed, with no immediate recollection of how he'd ended up there. As he tried to piece together the events leading up to his awakening, he discovered he still had one fake sideburn glued to his left cheek, and the bedazzled waistcoat of his costume was twisted uncomfortably and constricting his arm.

He realized there was someone in bed with him. He saw brunette hair poking out from under the covers, and everything clicked. The bartender — Jenny? Josie? Jeannie? She'd liked the Elvis bit and clearly hadn't gotten wind of the encore. He had been drunk as a skunk, over the deep end with cynicism and black, rock-bottom gallows humour. His spirits had been in the dumper; he'd honestly no longer given even one solitary fuck. As for her, she must have been sampling her own wares.

Surely, she was fifteen years younger than he, yet she had bought in. He vaguely recalled that something furtive and squishy had occurred.

Nervously scanning the unfamiliar room, he saw a white wicker table with photos on it and a dresser awash with ribbons and knick-knacks. Amongst the clutter were a pillbox hat and long white gloves. He dredged his foggy memory to haul up a conversational snippet. What was it? *Jackie O with a Q.* That was it: Jacquie. She stirred. He froze.

She rolled over and cracked her eyes a bit, mumbling vaguely in a croaky voice. Vicar looked at her and remembered that she was indeed quite lovely. Eyes set wide apart, high cheekbones, chestnut hair cut high at the back and longer in front, framing her chin and jaw perfectly. She looked remarkably like the real Jackie O, but with a streetwise look in her eye. He noticed her tattoos, too. Down the back, over the shoulder and upper arm, trailing off just above the elbow. Roses, birds, crests — he couldn't tell what the pattern was. Generally, he thought tattoos were deep regret waiting to happen, but he had to admit that hers did look awfully sexy.

Jacquie cleared her throat a couple of times and groaned. "Oh, my God! Did we really drink that much last night?"

Vicar responded dully, "Yes. I fear, yes." As his mind flashed back through the events of the night that he could recall, his face twitched with shame.

She let out a loud bark of laughter. "You scared everyone away. I've never seen anything like it. Awesome. They just didn't get it." At least she could appreciate the absurd.

He shifted his gaze away from her eyes and focused on the middle distance for a moment. "Yeah, they just didn't get it." *I am not sure I get it, either*, he thought.

"They thought it was going to be some stupid Elvis thing, but it was *ironic* Elvis. So cool. You were playing right over their heads!" Her loud laughter turned into a cough. She was awfully enthusiastic for someone who had just woken up, hungover, hard by a strange half-naked man.

He reflected briefly, feeling all the pieces in his mind rearrange to resonate with her interpretation. *Geez, maybe she's right.* Then he remembered the diarrhea attack and collapsed back to reality, feeling exactly like the old twenty-six-inch Magnavox he and his buddy had once heaved off a roof.

She rolled out of bed, revealing a figure that was knockout by anyone's standards. Really shapely and fit, with quite a bit of ink. Vicar blinked a couple of times, kicking himself that he'd bedded such a hottie but had no recollection of it. There were numerous tattoos and nuts and bolts sticking out of her in odd places, yet her demeanour was wholesome and cheerful — or at least it was first thing in the morning. He'd had no awareness of her piercings during the dark of night. Under the quilt he gently felt around to see if he had any lacerations.

She opened the venetian blinds and slid the window open, and as she turned, he saw yet another tattoo just below her bikini line: words inside a winged crest. Latin? Italian?

Conspicuously keeping his attention sharply focused on the words and not the surrounding area, he squinted and asked, "What does your tattoo say?"

She paused melodramatically and then fired back, her eyes glinting mischievously, "Abandon Hope, All Ye Who Enter Here."

Three / A Sign from Above

Vicar knew it was a walk of shame, but at least it possessed the charm of being a bizarre one. He plodded up the long rise on the road home that overlooked the Strait of Georgia, still Elvis, but minus the wig and the belt. Those were in a plastic grocery bag taken from Jacquie's kitchen drawer, dangling limply from his fingers. The hard glare of the morning sun made the water glint and the nearby islands stand out in stark relief. There were a few small craft flitting about, and one sailboat was into the wind, making good headway. It felt calm where he stood, but he saw some chop in the skinny. Probably a little bumpy. He crossed to the other shoulder to be that much closer to the beautiful view and felt his fuzzy brain clearing.

As he trudged up to the hill's crest, costumed as history's least successful hitchhiker, he was beginning the day already completely spent. He absently rummaged in the pocket of his preposterous trousers to be sure he had his phone. He longed for a good nap, maybe a snooze on the hillside.

A huge car appeared, rudely interrupting his tired, scratchy musings, veering recklessly into the oncoming lane, coming right at him. It was colossal and moving fast, on a direct course for him. He was a goner. Checkmate. Just like that, buh-bye. He couldn't even ditch to save himself; there was no foxhole, just a guardrail fencing off a sharp cliff with a twenty-foot drop down to the rocks.

With no other option apparent, he tensed up for his mortal end. Then the car, screeching, veered precipitously back to its proper lane. He perceived it in slow motion, mentally capturing the incident in black and white, like the snowy surveillance footage of a back-alley murder.

Shock and confusion swept over him as the car whizzed past, an arm's length away. The rogue car was empty, driverless, with no one visible inside it. It was something straight out of *Kolchak: The Night Stalker*. It was a stampeding horse, panicked, aimless, deadly, terrifying. Perhaps it had just rolled down the road, away from its parking spot?

He had been inches from certain death.

Vicar's head swivelled to follow the out-of-control monster, sure that it was about to plunge over the embankment to the rocky shore below. But, just then, he spied a tuft of white hair poking over the top of the seat. There was someone in the car. A person was behind the wheel and doing a very bad job indeed of helming the deadly black juggernaut.

In the pregnant seconds after the crisis, a cyclist cheerily glided over the hill and was confronted with the odd vision of Elvis, jaw agape, clutching a wig-stuffed grocery bag and gawking dumbly at a huge Fleetwood Brougham tacking into the distance. It was as if the car were a time machine that had just ejected its surprised emissary into this unlikely seaside location, far from the safety of Graceland.

The bicycle swished past as Vicar muttered, "Oh, my God. The King nearly flattened by a Cadillac. That has *got* to be a sign."

Four / Rah Rah Ross Poutine

"**J**esus Christ!" he barked at the traffic before him. There was always some dumb sonofabitch who felt he had to slow way down and swing wide into the right shoulder before making a left turn. "Whaddya pulling, a wagon?" he growled.

When the aimless beige Camry ahead of him finally cleared the shoulder, Ross Poutine put his foot to the floorboard, and the classic but showroom-shiny '66 Chevelle lit up instantly, ass drifting sharply, billowing smoke, chirping aggressively into second gear. By the time Mr. Geriatric Camry could even check his rearview mirror, Poutine was far down the road and up to a hundred clicks. *That's what 385 ponies will do for you*, he thought smugly.

He let off the gas and coasted down the hill to the little plaza where Liquor sat, the engine idling with a sound like shoes in a dryer. With a large arm crank he steered the expensive antique into the "reserved parking" stall and got out.

Before he could even get his key in the door, he had customers wanting booze at 9:30 in the morning. One of them was a regular, Mrs. Frankie Hall. She had painstakingly manoeuvred her car, which had been the pride and joy of her dearly departed husband, as close to the front door as she could get, then gotten her walker out of the cavernous back seat. Poutine looked at the wispy, birdlike woman standing next to the archaic, twenty-foot-long behemoth. She had a basket on her walker, and when she left it'd be full of wine. She was probably a hundred years old. She usually came in before noon on a Monday. It was very unusual for her to come on a Sunday, and so early in the day.

"Hello, there," she cackled, grinning at Poutine with the broad, old-timey charm of the Bowery Boys. With that, his earlier abrasive mood evaporated.

"Ready to tank up, Frankie?" he asked with affection.

"You betcha," she croaked. "Now, gimme some of the good stuff."

Poutine reached over to a rack and grabbed a huge box of wine. It was an astringent, cranky potion best consigned to a cauldron surrounded by witches with pricking thumbs, but it was cheap, and the box was an attractive fuchsia on black. He looked over his readers and asked, "Pinot, right?"

"That's what I've been missin'," Frankie yelled, grimacing as she futzed with her hearing aid. "Damn thing!" she cursed. "I can't hear a damn thing."

Poutine commiserated with a sympathetic cluck, laughed, and put the huge crate of cheap hooch into

Frankie's little basket. He held the front door open as she trundled out to her enormous Caddy, crinkling with amusement as he imagined the ninety-pound, hundred-year-old woman skippering that land yacht — that gigantic symbol of wealth and sophistication from another era — only to go home and crack into an economy box of cheap porch climber.

The locals knew Poutine through the shop windows; he was immediately recognizable even from a remarkable distance. There was really nobody else around who looked anything like him. You'd have had to go back at least forty years to find a suitable stand-in. His silhouette was era specific, and his was not the current era. It was not even three current eras ago, set end to end.

Like most of his ilk, somewhere around Grade 11 he'd found a look that was just rockin', and had stayed with it well into his fifties. The same look, no doubt, would accompany him to the grave: boot-cut Levi's jeans, matching Levi's jacket, denim shirt, black leather fanny pack. For fancy, he used a frilly tux shirt that he'd bought at Army & Navy in Gastown back in 1980. If it was good enough for Meat Loaf, it was good enough for him. He was a rebel, after all, presuming rebels grumbled about noise and watched *Wheel of Fortune*.

There was nothing either French or Russian about Poutine, but he sported a scraggly Irish wolfhound beard and ghastly, neglected *Aqualung* hair that had given genesis to his wry nickname. Born in Montreal, but resident on Vancouver Island for decades, he was a town fixture that some wit years ago had dubbed Ross Poutine. And, like his mystic Russian Orthodox namesake, he was known, jarringly, to smell like a goat, but no one could confirm if he owned one or it was just abysmal hygiene. His real name was McFaddish, Ross Fergus McFaddish, though faddish he most assuredly was not.

At first the young McFaddish had come out to the Island to be a logger, to chop down trees and make big money working for a big company that had big trucks. Ten hard years and two broken legs later, he'd gotten laid off, had gone on unemployment, then tried his hand at fishing. After his first paycheque, he'd seen pretty clearly that he was never going to get rich being a deckhand. He didn't know the first thing about boats, nor did he care to. He suffered terribly from what his ol' mum called *mal de mer*.

He liked cars. Muscle cars. Wide-tracked Pontiacs, six-packed Chryslers, steroidal Fords. But in his heart of hearts, he was a Chevy man. He'd never owned anything else, never even entertained the notion. His grandfather had been a Chevy man starting in 1927. His father was a Chevy man. He was a Chevy man. He'd driven west in 1972 in a '63 Impala, 283, 3-on-the-tree. Best car he'd ever owned. He winced at the thought of how he'd lost her.

He'd eventually tried selling cars, and for a season he ran the store down at the Tully Point dock. He'd even done a stint in the Hudson's Bay furniture department way down in Nanaimo. That had lasted about three months. None of the senior citizens wanted to buy their new chesterfield from a guy who smelled like he'd been fished out of a cesspool with a coat hanger, despite swinging past the men's cologne counter every morning to douse himself in Drakkar Noir.

Eventually, he opened Tyee Lagoon's only liquor store. He named it with the lone word *Liquor* after spending two weeks grinding his hardtack imagination to come up with a more colourful option. He'd thought You Liquor, You Brought Her was great, but his mother had been horrified when he told her. Not that he'd really given a shit what anyone thought, but a sign that long would have been expensive.

Liquor was the only place in walking distance to get booze. This was important because people always run out before they're satisfactorily pissed. Poutine appreciated drinking for the living it gave him. He adored driving for the pleasure it gave him. But even this self-appointed Rebel Without a Barber knew the stupidity in mixing the two. He'd learned it the hard way from the incident with his late Impala. Luckily, the only fatality had been a large Doug fir in the bush, and by the time he'd called a tow truck it was the next afternoon, after a nice nap and some bacon and eggs. To prevent that from happening way out here in Tyee Lagoon, he offered a booze delivery service to trusted customers. They ordered on the phone and he dropped it off. He'd made the judgment that it was better to fetch it to them than have them swerving all over fuck to come to his shop. Plus, drunk people tipped like sailors.

Five / Enter Liquor

Painters knew it as Capri blue, but the Vancouver Island sky above Tony Vicar was the same gorgeous cerulean he'd seen a thousand times before, and never once in the Mediterranean. It had a calming effect, giving him a feeling of comfort that soothed his unsettled mind and distracted him from the spectre of defeat that had lately hung over him. This year's warm season wasn't yet old enough to instill the sense of urgency he always felt in summer that he had to get to the beach now, because the good weather couldn't possibly last. No, not today. The shadows were just short enough to impart optimism for new undertakings and to foreshadow the dog days to come, or so he hoped.

As Vicar approached Liquor, he could see Ross Poutine inside, chatting with a poodle-haired customer who looked, Vicar thought, like a bloated Peter Frampton gone to seed. The door made a loud creak when he pulled it open. Poutine looked up, gave a tight smile, and nodded as the customer spoke.

"It was prolly forty pounds. Big fucker. Barely fit in my boat, dude."

"Mm-hmm," Poutine replied noncommittally. He had surely heard every bullshit fishing story ever told. Forty pounds meant ten pounds, and the guy had probably been afraid of it when he'd landed the damned thing. And the lying bastard drove a powder-blue Hyundai, to boot. Ee-yuck.

"Anywayzz," he said, "I see yuz got customers. It's been a slice, brah. I'll catch ya on the flip-flop."

Hearing this, Vicar grimaced and felt his shoulders go up. Slice? Flip-flop? What the hell? Why didn't he just put on a straw skimmer and say 23 skidoo? Vicar's revulsion of this guy was instinctive, yet he felt a moment of embarrassment as he caught Poutine noticing his response. As Poodle Hair turned to leave, Poutine looked again at Vicar, this time rolling his eyes.

As neutrally as he could, Vicar opened the conversation. "Telling you a few tall tales?" He expected Poutine to comment on the customer's buffoonish slang, but instead, he glanced out to the parking lot and replied, "Randy, dere? His boat. Ha, ha. He's homeless without a girlfriend."

Vicar wondered dryly if one could find girlfriends "on the flip-flop."

Poutine turned his attention to Vicar. "What can I do ya for?"

Vicar stated his case with clarity. "I need a job, and I'd like to apply for one here, if you have any openings."

Poutine's brow furrowed as he appraised Vicar. "You live round here. I seen you in here lotsa times."

"Yeah, I'm just down the road a little bit," Vicar replied agreeably. He held out his hand. "Tony Vicar."

"They call me Ross Poutine," he said, though every living soul in Tyee Lagoon knew his nickname. His hand was rough, dry, and powerful. "You got a driver's licence?"

"Yes," Vicar replied.

"Can you drive stick?"

"Yes."

"You gotta car?"

"Yes, I do." *Keep it simple.*

"What kinda car?"

"A Peugeot."

Poutine's head twisted away as he barked, "Ewww, fuck. A Poo-Joe? Seriously?"

Vicar looked at him with a mixture of disbelief and amusement. "Yeah, seriously. It's been a great car."

Poutine bent over and pretended to retch into the trash can. "What's it made of? Heineken cans?"

Hoping to moot the peripheral line of discussion, Vicar looked at him without expression and said, "Heineken is Dutch."

As if confessing from the depths of his heart, Poutine levelled, "I don't, ahh, like the Dutch cars, dere."

Vicar realized there could be no unknotting of the multiple skeins of cryptic illogic. "But you do have an opening?"

Poutine's tone softened, and he looked appraisingly at Vicar. A series of thoughts seemed to crawl across his face before he pivoted the conversation. "You look a lit-tle wrong in the tooth, dere."

Long. Long in the tooth. Vicar mentally corrected Poutine at the same instant that he felt the truthful sting of the observation.

"It's true. I am not a kid," he replied guardedly.

"Whaddaya, going through some stuff?" Poutine asked, suddenly solicitous, tender, disarming.

Vicar paused a moment, then dropped his guard a little. "Yes, it has been a challenging time," he admitted.

Poutine stroked his ghastly beard thoughtfully. Vicar looked closely at him and was hit by the stark contrast between his appalling appearance and the vibe of gentle concern that emanated from some unknown part of him. He was also hit by the dank tang of quadruped drifting from Poutine's direction.

"Well, one of the kids who was helping me is leavin' end of next week. I can't be here all the time, but the store's gotta be open irregardless."

Vicar again mentally corrected his grammar, feel-ing suddenly uncomfortable with this lopsided dynamic.

"Do you wanna come in next Monday? It should only take a coupla hours for you. But I had one kid who never got it. The whole thing was, ahh" — he paused to gather the words — "beneath his apprehension, dere."

Vicar looked up and to the right a little, accessing the part of his brain that might decipher that doozy. Click, click, click. Beyond his comprehension. *Oh God*, thought Vicar, *he's illiterate.*

Vicar cast his eyes over the equipment and shook his head. It was old, even by his standards. No wonder Poutine couldn't keep any kids in his employ. He might as well have had them shoeing horses out back. The most difficult part of this job was going to be constantly re-organizing the cooler as stock moved through.

"So, I guess you're not taking online orders, huh?" Vicar asked.

"Huh?"

"Online. Customers go to your website and place their orders …" He trailed off, realizing how ridiculous the question was.

"Huh?" This time Poutine's brow was crinkled in annoyance.

Glumly, Vicar envisioned himself blithely finding the right "flow" for the deck chairs on the Titanic. "Ross, buddy, you don't even take credit cards. You might as well be trading for pelts."

Poutine gruffly looked away.

Trying a new tack, Vicar said, "Young people don't even use the phone anymore."

Staring down at the counter, Poutine grumbled, "I'm going to reframe from comment."

Vicar instantly began to itch. He scratched his arm violently in response to this last malapropism.

The cash register had to go. The customer display had broken off numerous times and was held in place with yellowing Scotch tape. After a week in his new job, Vicar broke the news to Poutine, who was manhandling a heavy dolly stacked with champagne. He simply had to get a computer system. Vicar couldn't believe that he'd stayed afloat this long without one. Even geriatrics shopped on Amazon now.

Poutine had a big heart, but he was shipwrecked in a distant time. For him, the purchase of a new pair of pants would have been an emotional mountain to climb. It seemed, though, that for all his grumbling, he would have been happy to give the shop a facelift. He just didn't have the imagination, didn't know where to start. The whole concept aggravated him, wore on the tiny reserve of patience he had. Now, if somebody could have waved a magic wand and just made all that shit appear …

A few days later, and strongly against his will, Vicar was instructed to make a delivery in the precious Chevelle, to "keep up my image," Poutine insisted. It felt more like mounting an expedition; driving this car would be like attempting to saddle and break a rhino.

"Just go ginger with the gas, Tony, don't mat the whore, you'll be all over da place."

Vicar, stressed out and distracted, still spent an instant marvelling at Poutine's signature lingo.

"And watch the brakes. This baby's heavy, so she don' slow down so good. Gotta baby 'er a bit."

"Ross, I really don't feel safe in this thing. It's too much for me."

Too much for a grown man? Poutine looked aghast, as if Vicar had just requested a tender and loving hand job.

Vicar attempted to justify his reluctance. "I don't want to wreck your beautiful car."

"I don' want ya to wreck my beautiful car, either. But it's worth th' risk. Your car is for schoolgirls. You can't deliver booze in that damn Barbie Camper." He gestured dismissively at the blocky Peugeot.

Vicar sighed, trying to find the right angle of approach. "If I were to cause an accident while I was delivering for you, the store's reputation would be trashed. You'd lose all your delivery business." He knew his argument made no sense, but he was looking for any excuse not to use the Chevelle. He could not connect with Poutine's notion that booze had to be delivered in a muscle car.

"Don' gimme yer goddamn societal tissues, just git this booze over to Mrs. Hall's place on Sloop Road."

Vicar chuckled. Sometimes Poutine was so far off the mark that he did a spin-o-rama and nailed it by accident.

Poutine stood back, and Vicar, as advised, gingerly tapped the gas. Nothing happened. He tried again. Nothing. He looked questioningly at Poutine through the open window.

"Give 'er, ya fuckin' pansy!" Poutine admonished.

He put his foot down on the pedal and the big fat BF Goodrich 60s at the back left a streak of rubber thirty feet long, the car's rear end fishtailing as he desperately tried to keep the front wheels corrected. They both howled, Poutine with glee, Vicar with terror as he screamed onto the main road, nearly putting the car nose first into Mrs. Kanashiro's koi pond.

Vicar slowed down and rumbled menacingly toward his destination, trying to enjoy the spectacular view while wrestling with this, the most powerful car he'd ever operated. It was a beautiful showpiece, but about as relaxing as snakes in your sleeping bag. Its brakes may or may not have been functioning; it accelerated like the Space Shuttle or else didn't move at all. When it idled, it sounded like boulders in a cement mixer. It was ridiculous. What possible reason was there to use a car as powerful as a bulldozer only for light deliveries? Car guys were so weird, like gun guys, or airplane guys. Vicar didn't even think about including music guys.

The sky was puffy with low clouds moving noticeably at low altitude, but when he got to the bend with the good ocean view, he could see no whitecaps. Right above him was a huge, impressive-looking bird. It gracefully followed the Chevelle down the road. It was golden brown and had a massive wingspan. Juvenile bald eagle? Golden eagle? Bald eagles were abundant here, probably to the chagrin of American tourists, but he couldn't remember the last time he'd seen a golden; they came only to breed.

At the very top of the highest ground in town, on a switchback curve leading to what must have been the deadliest driveway turnoff in all Tyee Lagoon, he found the house of Mrs. Frankie Hall. He rolled down her driveway and pulled up near the garage door.

An elderly man with a splotchy tan and the skinniest legs Vicar had ever seen answered her door. He wore tight beige shorts hiked up to his nipples. His balls were hanging out one leg hole, dripping down like a long thread of sap covered in pine needles. Vicar didn't know how to react when he saw the dangling tackle.

As Frankie Hall slowly shuffled to the door, purse in hand, she saw his surprise and deduced the problem.

"Oh, Pasquale, your whatnots are showing again," she said chirpily, pronouncing it Pusk-Wally. She turned to Vicar with a lopsided grin and stage-whispered, "I call him the Sack of Rome."

Vicar presented her wine in a box.

"Could you just take it into the garage, dear? There's a shelf for my hooch. You'll see it there."

Smiling, Vicar said, "Of course, of course."

Upon entering the huge garage, he found the parked hulk of the longest black Cadillac he'd ever seen. *Amend that*, he twigged, *I saw it once before, when it almost killed me.*

He reported back to Frankie when he was done. Glancing at her white hair, he realized that it was she who'd so badly navigated the huge death ship when it had nearly sunk him.

"Here you are, dear." She handed him a tip.

Vicar stood there for just a moment and then said, "That big old Cadillac looks hard to get in and out of the garage. Do you drive it very often?"

"Oh no, I only go out once in a while."

"Hmm, I have a feeling it might go through gas pretty quickly."

"Well, it ain't no economy car," she quipped brightly.

"Tell ya what, Mrs. Hall, I have a proposition for you. If you call me down at Liquor, I can run all your deliveries up here, not just your vino. Your groceries or maybe something from the drugstore. It might be a lot easier than driving. Anything you need."

"Well, isn't that nice, but I already have a boy-friend." She crooked her thumb over her shoulder toward

Pasquale, who had shuffled to the counter and was currently trying to outsmart the lid of a coffee can.

"No, ma'am. I don't mean it that way, although now that you mention it, it is mighty tempting." He winked outrageously at her, and she glowed in response. "I just think that your car is awfully large, and your needs are probably pretty small. Someone from the shop drives past here several times a day. You just call me, and we'll drop stuff up here, no problem. 'Kay?"

She patted his hand gently. "Shall do, handsome," she flirted through the crack of the door, obviously pleased, as Vicar looked down at his seventy-five-cent tip.

A lovely, wholesome girl with Margaret Keane big eyes and carefully plaited strawberry hair sweetly answered the door. Tony Vicar's mind flashed back to Grade 7, when his heart had melted at the sight of a classmate who'd looked much like her. He had given up hope that young ladies like this still existed and half expected Huck Finn to peek out from behind her.

Instead, a man padded out from a side room. It was that poodle-haired surf bum from the other day, flashy sunglasses pushed up on his forehead. Ol' Catchya on the Flip-Flop. What was it? Randy? With one limp hand, he took delivery of the wine, and with the other, weakly grasped Vicar's fingers in an overtly stylized, unnecessary greeting, like a self-appointed Sultan of Skeeve in a receiving line. "I just gotta get my cash, dude. Hang tight." Infuriatingly, he said *dude* with a raspy, affected, faux-Californian drawl. Vicar's eyes began to water slightly at the sound of his voice.

Randy the Poodle poked around, presumably looking for his missing wallet. He barked crudely for Becky, the girl who had answered the door. Vicar blinked once or twice … her name was actually Becky. How strange. Becky with the Good Hair, mused Vicar, but Randy with the Weak Handshake. He was riffing poorly as a result of the uncomfortable feeling in the house; he was put off by the mere sight of the man. Through bedrock belief, passed down from father to son for many generations in his lineage, Vicar knew with certainty that a wet-fish grasp portended wickedness.

Becky timidly presented herself, and Randy made a show of giving her hell for moving his wallet while she mumbled vain protests. Vicar felt the whole performance was for his benefit. The poodle-coiffed dick lecturing that young, sweet snapshot of Vicar's youth was the embodiment of layabout boyfriend masquerading as stepdad. He was showing off his power over the defenceless to a total stranger who waited uncomfortably at the door to be paid so he could just get outta there.

Finally, Randy spied the missing wallet over on the kitchen counter. Grabbing it, he checked its contents and accused her of getting light-fingered with his cash. Her mother came creeping in, her eyes frightened, looking bedraggled and — oddly for this time of day — wearing a tattered terry housecoat large enough to use as a boat tarp. Vicar noticed a chopstick in her hair holding up her bun. Young Becky's eyes flicked over to Vicar in embarrassment as Randy the Increasingly Offensive Surfer Poodle amped up his tirade.

"I want to talk to you outside. Right now."

Becky followed compliantly, shuffling past with her eyes cast down. Vicar deliberately fixated on the chopstick to ignore the pall of awkwardness that fell on the scene. The mother gazed past him and chewed her lip nervously. Behind him he heard muttering. Randy the Poodle Douche raised his voice and began to sound very aggressive. Alarmed, Vicar stepped back from the door and turned toward them to see what domestic mess was brewing up.

Young Becky was finally getting angry at her treatment, and she raised her voice. "*No*, I did not take your money! Leave me alone, Randy." Her strawberry plaits twisted as she shook her head, face flushing, voice shrill with apprehension. Randy, blithely unaware that he was one bad decision away from entering a deadly situation, grabbed Becky by the arm and started shaking her roughly, a truly ominous glare on his face.

Vicar watched with surging anxiety for a moment as klaxons went off in his brain. "Let her go!" he commanded sharply.

Randy with the Poor Hair and Poorer Judgment rounded on him. "Get the fuck off my property, you sonofabitch. This is none of your fuckin' business." His eyes looked psychotic. It was as if someone had flipped a switch in Randy, turning him from laughable caricature to monster with one click. Vicar's senses were ratcheted sky high, and he thought he could see watery, unpleasant colours swirling around this guy's face. Vicar was like that sometimes.

He put his hands up, palms out, but stood his ground. "Let her go and calm down, and then I'll leave."

Randy released his grip on Becky, approached threateningly, and growled, "You'll leave *now*."

Still maintaining his ground, with his torso twisted, his right arm slyly cocked back, Vicar spoke with menacing calm. "No real man roughs up a little girl. You wanna dance with me, you cocksucker?"

Poodle Hair sneered and reached toward Vicar, saying, "Chillax, brah," with venom.

The word *chillax* triggered a full-on rage in Vicar. No grown man who used that bastardized pseudo-word could go without ruthless punishment. It indicated a wilful embrace of cultural retardation, of linguistic vandalism that was bringing society down to unsustainably Kardashian levels. Randy the Human Poodle illustrated his vileness with that one odious utterance. And, oh yeah, he also beat up girls. The order was given: *Smite the filthy cur.*

Vicar lashed out powerfully, the heel of his hand smashing at Randy the Speed Bag right under the nose, nearly shearing it right off his stupid face. The hit was terrible, a thunderous knockout blow, with shoulder, hips, knees, and ankles leveraging its fierce impact. Vicar followed through like George Foreman, his body bent over halfway, his arm extended as he connected.

Randy the Frizzy-Wigged Crash Test Dummy rocketed backward, brutally cracking his head on the sharp corner of the wall, and hemorrhaging all over his very own custom-made Peckinpah tableau. His ridiculous yacht rock aviator shades flew off in a high parabola, clattering down into a spreading pool of red next to his too-seldom-used head.

Mother and daughter gasped and then stood in silent awe for several heartbeats. The mother began sobbing. Calmly, Vicar smoothed his jacket and looked down at the bleeding, unconscious turd at his feet. He said quietly, "I am chillaxed."

Officially, she was Constable Hayley Constanz, but her pals all called her Con-Con. She knew practically everyone in town pretty well.

"What happened?" She was simple and direct without any of the formality police normally used in such a situation.

"He was roughing up the girl, Becky. I stopped him."

Con-Con dropped her head and turned it sideways. "Oh, you stopped him, all right," she said wryly. "He spent the night in the hospital."

"Good," Vicar said.

"You realize you could end up in a lot of trouble, Tony?"

"Yeah, but I'd rather deal with that than be the chickenshit who watched an innocent girl get roughed up."

She glanced up as impassively as she could manage and tried to stay professional. Con-Con was already almost six feet in her stocking feet; with her forage cap on, she was even taller. One of the few Mounties around and the only one born in Tyee Lagoon, she had somehow finally gotten a posting here, after stints in Nunavut and the most barren stretches of Northern Saskatchewan. She lived close by her mother, who peppered her voice mail with messages along the lines of, "Please tell Hayley her mother called."

She'd tried to teach her mother how to text, but it was hopeless. Mom could seldom locate the cellphone, and when she did, the battery would be dead, or she wouldn't be able to find her readers to see the keypad, or she'd get flustered and call 911 by accident. How had she ever worked a job and raised a daughter all by herself out here in the country? Now she couldn't even work the TV remote.

"So, how did it go down?" Con-Con asked. Vicar told her, in a precise and economical manner. She took notes, once or twice asking for clarifications and murmuring "Mm-hmm."

About ten minutes later, she said, "He claims you attacked him, and it was unprovoked."

"Con-Con," Vicar said defensively, "he is a douchebag. He told me to *chillax*."

"Ah." She pursed her lips. "Not sure that's a reason to give a guy brain damage."

"If he uses that word he's already brain damaged," he shot back.

"You might wanna watch what you say during your statement, Tone." Her chuckle was a warning.

"Is he actually brain damaged?"

Concern flooded his face. Seeing this, Con-Con's tone changed. She let her face soften.

"How in the hell could anyone tell?" she muttered derisively. "We'll have to see, I guess. Look, thanks for your co-operation." She put her notebook back into her shirt pocket.

"Am I in trouble?" he asked.

"Well, he may want to press charges, and his face is pretty good evidence against you at this point. It's going to be some time before he can stop and smell the roses." She raised her eyebrows, gave him a tight, curt smile, and departed.

Eight / Hardware Store Epiphany

Vicar lumbered into Lagoon Hardware Store like a persecuted bear, licking a chocolate-dipped cone and not giving a shit about the sign that said, *No Food Please*. The cashier looked apprehensively at his ice cream. Vicar gave her a flinty stare, fairly begging her to say something. But she demurred, and he wandered slowly down the paint aisle.

There, to his right, was a salesclerk. It was the lady in dusty-rose chiffon from the wedding, that awful wedding — the lady who couldn't keep time. She was yet another reminder of how slippery his slope seemed to be. He rounded the corner behind her and watched dully as she awkwardly demonstrated how to use "the Clapper" with a bedroom lamp. She vainly clapped and clapped and clapped, growing increasingly flustered.

Vicar ambled along the side window that looked out on the roundabout, where some newspaper boxes stood unevenly in the gravel. "Dozens Dead in Mumbai Terrorist Blast," a headline blared. The photo provided grisly details that made him wince.

He absently licked the drips from his ice cream and saw a competing headline on the local rag alerting everyone: "Winds Damage Kiosk." There was an accompanying low-res snapshot of a dishevelled roadside produce hut. It featured the hangdog owner in a hellish checked shirt pointing at a highlighted circle of missing roofing shingles. Vicar hacked out a guffaw of sheer disbelief and felt a sudden, profound cognitive dissonance.

His vision blurred, and his hearing shut down.

■ ■ ■

He is suddenly in a cavern, watching flickering images projected onto its walls. They show brief flashes of misery — plagues, bloodshed, cruelty, roving gangs of unhinged skinheads, auto-tuned vocalists, venal politicians, miracle diets, Kool-Aid-swilling cults, and Real Housewives of various and sundry places: things life has meted out with smiling malevolence to man and beast alike. Nobody really takes any notice; it's all just curling wallpaper randomly plastered to the insides of their heads. He absently wipes his sticky fingers on the seam of his pants.

Too many fixate on fictional junk. They go around and around and around. Their philosophy — if they have one — is based on price, but seldom on value. They get up at 6:00 a.m., to save twelve cents a pound on tomatoes, driving for two hours in their Bimmers to greedily snatch up a few. They aspire to extremely tidy driveways. They spend far too many Saturdays setting their belongings at right angles to show their dominion over chaos, as if that is a thing. They spend days edging their lawns to make perfectly straight lines when they could instead be talking to their kids about the history of the world and how it reveals the future. They speculate endlessly about royal engagements and celebrity divorces at their neighbours' weekend mixers, spending far more time gathering intelligence than imparting knowledge. They are convinced that boldly stating an opinion is more important than understanding its ramifications. They distrust imagination because it is not graphable.

They are the tactical rich — skinflint millionaires ravaging the Sally Ann, reselling their bargain booty on eBay for maximum profit, poring over flyers in order to be the early bird amongst a horde of lemmings. Life can be depicted on a balance sheet, after all. This is war, economic Darwinism, and they are at the apex. They wouldn't leave a good tip for a waiter who had donated them an organ.

Vicar realizes how rewarding unoriginality can be and feels encircled by blank, desolate mediocrities bereft of talent or vision — high-status garbage pickers.

He slowly pirouettes, trancelike, in the alcove near the paint rollers. Shoppers muscle past. One truculent lady bumps him with her buggy and pretends it was an accident. He doesn't even acknowledge her as she rolls by, despite the biting honk of her perfume hanging around her like a cloud of DEET. Somehow her rank passage seems perfectly timed.

His mind is gyrating now, spitting out examples to buttress his case. The images now flood the cavern. A roiling cataract is unleashed.

He stares at a thirty-dollar packet of spot remover; Lady Macbeth's favourite, no doubt. How immaculate do they require things to be? These people buy crap and then spend nearly all their time cleaning it. My God! They are janitors who think they can buff and polish their way to providence. They call it "protecting their investment," as if there were some mojo in a highly burnished gas barbecue that will inoculate them against their own banality.

His head is down now, shaking slowly back and forth. One of the apron-clad employees leans into the aisle and peers at him suspiciously. Vicar puts a hand to his forehead and feels a familiar headachy gloom creep up his neck toward his temples.

All the catastrophic hazards the human race has fought: smallpox, diphtheria, cholera, black plague, typhus, leprosy, and polio. Then, suddenly, lacking a challenge, we lose our minds over things like gluten. He imagines her, that evil demoness, Gluten, taking on multi-limbed form: the Bringer of Bloating. Before her, a field of kneeling trophy wives in perfectly fitting two-hundred-dollar jeans and superb shoes avert their flawlessly threaded brows from her blinding power. The Great Gluten holds a mobile phone in each hand, sending texts at a ferocious speed. The throng struggles to reply with novel emojis that will please her sufficiently to save themselves from doom and water retention. In the cheap seats far away from all the hubbub, the genuine celiacs sit despondent, hidden from sight by the faddish throng who study them with aspirations of someday feigning perfectly the disease that true sufferers so hate.

Vicar replays the vicious knockout he delivered to Randy the Vile Poodle and tries to make sense of it. He knows the feckless fop deserves it and, oh, so much more, but he can't understand why no one else ever acted, or why he was incapable *of not acting, no matter the personal cost. The passivity of people stumps him. The need to act is as obvious as picking up a piece of trash on the floor in front of you or holding the door for the person behind you. Clear, normal, correct, appropriate — no-brainer stuff. Something within him stirs. No, damn it. He is not wrong. He* can't *be wrong, can he?*

– – –

Vicar rocketed up from the depths of his cavern and was again in the hardware store. His ice cream had dripped all over the floor, a gooey illustration of why the sign was on the door in the first place. He banged down the mucky cone and spun on his heel. As he glided past the huffing, arrhythmic clerk at the counter fruitlessly swatting her hands together, he clapped sharply exactly once, and lo, the light bulb turned on.

– – –

Under his own initiative, Vicar attempted to tackle creating a website for Liquor, but came to a halt early on. Staring at the screen, utterly confused, he suddenly sympathized with Poutine's dim view of technology. "Goddamn gadgets" was Poutine's only response besides angry scowling, which wasn't any help. Vicar was beginning to suspect his modernization efforts would get him fired, and he was desperate for the income.

Off the top of his head, the only person he knew who might understand all this claptrap was Jacquie O, and at any rate, it gave him a legit reason to call her. He reached for the lone phone on the premises: an ancient, chipped artifact from the late twentieth century, orange in colour and liberally spattered with expectorated food chunks and black grime. He gingerly picked it up with his fingertips and held it an inch from his ear as he looked at the number Jacquie had written on the back of an old recycling schedule.

Vicar dialed Jacquie's number and looked at Poutine. "I'm going to get some help with this website, then I'm going to force you to upgrade this Stone Age junk!"

From across the shop, Poutine looked over his glasses and scowled in displeasure, but said nothing.

Vicar got her voice mail. He nervously left a message at the beep. "Uhhh, hi, Jacquie, it's, ahhh, Tony Vicar calling. I'm just down here at Liquor, trying to set up a website, and I'm a bit, ahh, stumped. I wonder if you know anything about this stuff. Ahhh, you mentioned that you've done some website work. Ahh, gimme a call, please." He left his number twice, reciting it with extravagant clarity.

His nose sensed Poutine's odoriferous approach.

"Aha," Poutine uttered with warming interest, "sounds like you're hot for that one."

Vicar was taken aback. "What? It's just someone I met recently."

"Yeah, yeah." Poutine laughed. "Mr. Bossy Boots with the goddamn computer, dere. Gotta bring in yer girlfriend fer help. Better buy some quiche. I'll come in here and she'll be kickin' yer ass and you'll be in the feeble position."

Vicar burst out laughing.

Jacquie was curled up on the couch, the phone to her ear. "Mm-hmm. Mm-hmm. Uh-huh ... Mom, you've told me at least fifty times. I know."

Her mother, alone and far away, was perennially concerned that her beautiful daughter was going off the rails. First, she'd started dancing naked for money like some common hussy, and then she'd kept company with a string of men, most of them old farts.

"The last one, that Prentiss ... I told you he was bad news."

"He was a lovely guy. He died. He really couldn't help it."

"Couldn't he have bought a car like everyone else? Who dies on a bicycle, for God's sake? Didn't he care about leaving you behind with a broken heart? Is that all we O'Neil women can ever look forward to?"

Jacquie felt herself getting aggravated, then thought

better of it and started laughing. "I swear I still don't know when you're kidding ..."

"Oh, never mind. Sometimes I don't know myself. Now this new one, what's he like?"

"Uhh, not too sure. I'm just getting to know him."

"You call me to tell me you're seeing someone? But you don't know him? He's probably another one of your grandpa types. Did you already bonk him?"

"Mom!"

"He must have quite the unit."

"Mom!"

"Does he need blue pills?"

"MOM!"

▄ ▄ ▄

Vicar stacked a display of Malbec in the corner. The shop door opened, and two people walked in. He was deep in thought about the dark, angry edge that had invaded his existence, and so it took a moment for him to recognize them as Becky and her mother. He looked at them warily but welcomed them into the store all the same.

The girl fidgeted with something in her hands. After some awkward pleasantries, her mother said, "We just want to thank you."

"Thank me?" He was confused.

"Yes, he's been awful to Becky. Well, to both of us ... This isn't the first time ..." She looked down.

Vicar appraised them solemnly for a heartbeat and said, "Well, I'm the one who's sorry, actually. I just snapped when I saw what he was doing to you." He knew it was only partially true. He'd snapped all right, but his frustration had been mounting for years.

"Mom kicked him out," Becky began confidently, then grew soft and frightened. "I'm really scared of him." Her voice sank down to a near whisper. "He hit Mom that day, too."

Unable to censor himself, Vicar blurted, "Aw, fuck." He began to apologize for his language, but the mother stopped him.

"We've wanted out for a long time," she said. "You forced me to finally do what I should have done a long time ago."

Vicar stood there, hands instinctively covering his genitals, feeling as if he were naked in a courtroom.

Becky stepped forward and extended her hand, which held a glittering object. "This is for you. It's a halo because you were our guardian angel."

He took the garland and tinfoil halo from her and grasped her hand tenderly, deeply moved. A tear sprang to his eyes, and he mumbled, "Thank you, thank you."

— — —

"Okay, now when you scan the bottle, it finds the price for you and puts it up here on the screen," Jacquie said. "Also, it changes the stock quantity, so you'll know you need to replace it next time you order. For stock, you press here." The screen flashed to all the stock in a quick blink.

Poutine hunched over the new monitor, utterly entranced, muttering in sheer wonder, as if he were watching the very birth of life in the galaxy. Vicar stood behind the two of them, feeling the gravitational pull of Jacquie's marvellous ass, but still managing to pay attention. She passed a little book to Vicar that contained notations written in her hand of all the usernames, passwords, and special codes they'd need to learn.

"Put this in a safe place, gentlemen."

Poutine straightened up. "Safety deposit box?"

She laughed. "No, no! Just a drawer or someplace you can't lose it. If you have to log in or change passwords, this will be your bible."

Poutine snatched it out of Vicar's hand and reverently put it in a locking drawer next to what appeared to be an old-fashioned belt-mounted mechanical change dispenser.

Poutine stood back from all the new equipment and glanced at the glamorous website displayed on one of the monitors. He paced out to the middle of the store, gazed upon the new equipment with pride, then walked to the side and looked at it from yet another angle. He was as delighted as Vicar had ever seen him. He made a showy jog back to the staff room and returned quickly.

"Now you take that filly out for some fancy grub," he said, gesturing at a smiling Jacquie as he put a fistful of cash in Vicar's hand. He was jarringly out of step with the times, but a gentleman all the same, and he was clearly grateful for all the help. It looked like he was misting up a little. He dabbed his eye with a tattered cuff and sniffed.

Vicar, surprised at Poutine's show of emotion, looked down at his hand and was about suggest his boss come along, too, when he realized that the pong surrounding Poutine would make eating dinner impossible. The man was incredibly kind, yet also incredibly stinky. And, so, Vicar simply accepted.

Ten / Night of the Living Dead

Caoilfhoinn Jacqueline O'Neil, known generally as Jacquie O, never used her first given name. No one could spell it, and few could extract *Key-Linn* from *Caoilfhoinn*. Even she herself had misspelled it on occasion, embarrassingly. It had been a tip of the hat to her Irish grandfather, but she felt very little connection to the name or the culture, other than the deep tingling she felt when Celtic music began to drone, making her desperate for a pint. But she was Canadian. There was nothing unique about liking those things here.

She entered Tony Vicar's tiny house and gawked openly at the sea of bric-a-brac that crowded it. His balled-up Elvis costume, hiding amongst the dust bunnies, where laundry lay in several piles, gave the room a discouraging air. The small house overflowed with random pieces of ill-matched furniture clearly collected over a lifetime of bachelorhood. *What a hodgepodge*, she thought.

A gorgeous, elegant sideboard and four kitchen chairs — one nice, three cracked and wobbly. A beige La-Z-Boy clearly retrieved from a pile in a lane was positioned in the dead centre of the room. A table presumably heisted from the set of *The Golden Girls* was rammed in a corner. And all was set against an audio system straight out of mission control at the Jet Propulsion Laboratory.

Speakers surrounded the little room, powered by towers of things she couldn't identify that blinked and were covered with knobs. It all looked like a slob's space-ship. How was it that men could obsess over the tiniest detail of a woman's anatomy, yet happily live in the contents of an overturned dump truck? If ever there were a house that needed a woman's touch, it was this one.

Vicar waved an aerosol can around just ahead of her in the vain hope of disguising the stale male odour. *Ugh. Now it smells like somebody shat Banff.*

Everything was covered in magazines, seashells, old chunks of rock, unopened mail, antique tourist souvenirs, and dirty dishes. There was a small diploma so faded that she couldn't make out the writing on it in the oblique light, guitars and their cases leaning against every verti-cal surface, books stacked up the far wall to eye level, a large mounted print of some man holding a saxophone, a giant statue of a dinosaur that came from Drumheller, an accordion, a colour picture of Earth, and two or three vintage pinups. The pinups interested her, so she strolled over to inspect them.

The pine-fresh scent settled upon her like a sylvan glade of nausea. Breathing into her sleeve for momen-tary relief, she began her research. "Have you ever been married?" The answer was starkly apparent, yet strangely, she felt nervous asking.

"No. No. Close, but no cigar," Vicar said glibly. "I'm told I am too hard to live with, but I disagree. I just like my space."

Jacquie turned to meet his gaze, then swiftly surveyed the jumbled scene before her and suppressed a chuckle.

"So, when did you start DJing?" she asked, gently guiding the conversation away from matrimony.

"When I lost my job."

"Doing what?" she asked.

"Most recently I sold stereos." He waved his arm at the equipment taking up his living room. "But I play in bands on the weekends, too."

"Oh, yah," she replied with a Canuck glottal stop, "any bands I might know?" She suddenly sounded so young.

He looked up and put his hand to his chin. "Uhh, Fibreglass Tigress? Prog Rock. Pete had a gong. Pretty cool. No? What about Lady in Her Eighties? Loverboy Tribute. I had red leather pants." He started singing. "She's turning on the heating pad, she's got phlebitis a touch … Oooh and she's a million above … Hot flashin' love!"

Jacquie's eyes widened as she leaned imperceptibly away from him.

"Not that one either? Hmmm. The Wizards of Awz-Some? Lots of Elton John. The old stuff, before he started singing about the Circle of fucking Life," Vicar said sagaciously. "What about the Artificial Hip? That's our tribute to the Perennially Hip, who are a tribute to the Tragically Hip. We had a great show at Memorial Hall two years ago — we rented this *huge* light show and the same PA that Trooper used the night before."

He went on at some length about wattage, something called a "sage plot" or maybe "stage pot," the band members' nicknames (Tin Ear was one that stuck in her memory) and monitor problems — it sounded like he'd said "feet-back" (but that was anatomically impossible, wasn't it?). She could barely understand him. He was babbling at top speed, assuming she understood all his lingo. He added an unrelated sidebar about an amplifier borrowed from someone named Zonk.

He then climaxed with a well-rehearsed set piece about the song they'd dedicated to a buddy who had just lost a hundred pounds after a two-year-long diet. It was a send-up called "Lou Ortiz Is Shrinking But I Don't Want to Slim." Hi-*lar*-ious, of course.

She nodded her head, gamely trying to follow along, but losing the thread as he trilled in a tangential flare-up of exuberance.

"You still play, don't you?" she asked, hoping to redirect the flow of his outburst. His boyish enthusiasm was not what attracted her, so she focused on his grey temples.

"Uhh, yeah, I just can't keep a group together. No one will commit and take it to the next level. People just don't get it."

She nodded sympathetically but didn't really relate. Even a complete fool would have given up such fantastic pipe dreams twenty-five years ago. It was suddenly a drab line of discussion.

Vicar looked at her and said, "Didn't you say you did some dancing to put yourself through school?"

"I was a stripper," she said, not obscuring the job description with any fancy wordplay.

"Really? And you put yourself through school that way?"

"The money was pretty good. I took classes all day and danced three nights a week at Beaver Fever in Victoria. I did this sixties Jackie thing — Coco Chanel outfit with the pillbox hat and the long white gloves. Classy. Vintage." She glanced at his pinups on the wall. "Like that." She pointed at a nude shot of Marilyn Monroe poolside.

Vicar looked at her for a few seconds, trying to conjure the scenario. It was a complete cliché, impossible to believe.

"And you became a crusading lawyer, now offering services *pro bono* to the starving and huddled masses," he quipped.

"No, you rude bastard," she shot back, laughing. "I was taking psychology."

At that his face screwed up in a comedic grimace. "Cake Decorating 101."

She frowned. "I quit after my third year. It was kinda pointless. I was treading water. I'll go back and finish someday, but the world doesn't need an exotic-dancing psychologist." She realized she was justifying her educational inadequacies to a greying, barely employed man who got excited about tribute bands.

Vicar, switching unpredictably back to being intelligent and thoughtful, asked, "Are you sure about that? It would give you a lot of street cred." He mentally listed all the regular, not particularly sophisticated people he knew who could use a down-to-earth, sympathetic ear from someone who'd tasted life on the edgier side. "Some people won't get counselling because they think their problems would never be understood by some highfalutin shrink in a cardigan."

He thought about it for a second and knew he would have sought help if he had ever gotten in over his head. He was sure of it, even though he wasn't mushy, didn't enjoy talking about feelings, and had never had much luck with girlfriends because he always seemed to pick the ones who preferred to bathe in a pool of undirected emotion. He thought about the one who had broken out in a two-day crying jag over onion rings versus French fries. He'd said to her, "You can't win an argument with logic, so you're left with weeping and manipulation." And that was it. She'd chucked him out, and he'd departed with barely disguised delight.

Jacquie stayed quiet and thoughtful. Vicar was looking more toward her than at her, but even so, he could see a kindness, a warm, suffusing aura that belied the tattooed epigram on her mons veneris and which put her in electric bas-relief like he was seeing her through an old View-Master. *There's something about this one*, he thought. He changed the subject.

"You want a glass of wine and some tunes?" He turned to the sideboard, which contained bottles with surprisingly high-quality labels.

"Sure," she said agreeably.

"What would you like to listen to?" The question was only perfunctory. He didn't give a shit what civilians listened to.

"Something with a cool mood. Do you have any Lil Wayne?"

Deadpan, he replied, "Yes. I have a great version of 'Danke Schoen, Live at the Sands,'" His wisecrack was lost on her.

He struck a match to a large scented candle, then picked up the remote control and started a track. He ceremoniously passed Jacquie a glass of red wine and lowered himself almost reverently into his big chair as Tommy Banks's piano began "My Old Flame." It drifted soothingly toward him; hearing it was like being plunged into a hot massaging spa after spending two days shovelling gravel. Vicar felt a little catch in his throat when the martini-dry tone of PJ Perry's alto sax entered at the top of the verse. *Ahh*, he exulted, *the sound of true masters*.

Jacquie listened to all of fifteen seconds of the track. "This is boring," she said dismissively.

Vicar's head snapped left, and he cartoonishly widened his eyes. "Shut that cakehole and listen."

She jumped back, shocked, though he knew she could tell he was only joking. After a moment he struck a new tone.

"You're a dancer. Visualize this as a dance. The alto sax is some romantic reliving a memory."

She looked doubtful, but curious.

"Close your eyes, take a breath, and let go."

She did as instructed.

After a minute he asked, "What do you see?"

"I see the figure of a man wearing white tails and spectator shoes. I can't see his face. He's moving with the melody, almost flying. Who is the piano?" she asked softly now, getting into it.

"You decide."

"I decide?" She exhaled slowly.

At the end of the phrase, the sax played a little fill, just a bit of air fah-fah-fuffing gently out of the mouthpiece. Zoh doh du bee-ahh. Wordlessly, the sweet, reedy voice confided; Vicar heard its wistful longing.

"I see a nighttime skyline, the silhouette of a dancer gliding in front of it, soft lighting."

He grinned. *Another convert*, he thought. Jacquie seemed to be thrilled with the visions, as though he'd just reached over and plugged in a light within her brain. She was so excited she let out a little squeak.

— — —

Dinner options were severely limited. Next to a gas station currently out of business and the local sex shop, Sir Vic's, there was the pancake house, which had used to be the Dominion Luncheonette. That wasn't gonna cut it.

They rattled down the road in Vicar's red car, which was proudly bedecked with the garland and tinfoil halo; it had been lovingly affixed with gaff tape and a heavy magnet.

He screwed up his face as he mused about the limited dining options. Jacquie cheerfully offered, "There's a new place called Buffet Delirante right by the chiropractor. Let's give that a try. It's fusion cuisine."

He began to regret their choice the instant they left the gravel plaza and entered the premises. All the surfaces were white, shiny, and hard. The lighting and echo and stainless-steel tubes supporting everything made the place feel like a laboratory, or an operating theatre. It was fusion, all right — a marriage of sterile and unwelcoming. It had all the warmth of a North Korean prison cafeteria, and the sight of a muddy pickup truck out the front window was jarring. It was as if they'd suddenly been abducted by aliens hovering over a rock quarry and beamed into their saucer.

They stood in the entrance for several long moments, being ignored in a restaurant completely bereft of customers apart from them. Vicar's hackles were starting to rise when a young woman finally strolled to the hostess desk.

Her voice came smack dab out of the dead centre of the millennial generational shift. Her vocal fry was so pronounced that Vicar was sure she had swallowed a kazoo. She glanced down at her reservations screen, then looked at them, seemingly inconvenienced. "Zzzxxx, zzzxxxkkkarrrgh?"

Vicar looked at Jacquie and then back at the young woman. "I'm sorry?" he asked, genuinely at a loss as to what she had just hacked up at him.

Her head made a little twist of impatience, and she repeated, "Zzzxxx, zzzxxxkkkarrrgh?" This time the uptalk at the end made it clear that she'd asked a question.

Vicar paused for several moments with his mouth slightly open. "Would you like a lozenge?"

With that, Jacquie stepped in and started frying up some variety of verbal concoction herself. Vicar watched and listened, befuddled, as Jacquie gargled her words just like the hostess. They might as well have been speaking Low Dutch during a root canal. The two women appeared to achieve a kind of concordance.

After they were seated, Vicar looked around at the clinical décor and said dryly, "Well, isn't this cozy? What language was that you were speaking, by the way?"

"This is going to be a rough dinner, isn't it?" Jacquie asked.

"No, no." Vicar told himself to turn the page. "Now that we're here, let's have something delicious."

Jacquie looked at him, probing his eyes. "Yes, yes, I peeked at the menu — looks good. I wonder if they have any specials?"

"You know, ol' Ross really lit up when he saw all that equipment working as advertised. You did a helluva job, Jacquie."

Her eyes twinkled as she looked up. "You're welcome, Tony. It's nice getting to know you."

If this was turning out to be a courtship, they were going about it bass-ackwards, Vicar realized — sex first, dinner second.

Something in his mind suddenly said *The Ipcress File*. He craned his neck around and was rewarded with the sight of Michael Caine's eyeglasses from said film adorning a twit who must have stolen his baby brother's pants and then waded through a lake. He held huge menus before him as if they were holy tablets, brought down from on high. The tendrils of his foot-long beard could have won a topiary trophy at the Hampton Court Palace Garden Festival.

Vicar forced a smile and dutifully followed along while the waiter made his pitch. The menu was covered in exotic descriptors gratuitously diacritical and absent of meaning. Since when did *potato* need an umlaut? He started losing interest quickly.

Oblivious, Michael Caine's eyewear stunt double went on at some length about the *carte du jour* and how to read it, with the implication that what he grandly called the "menu-browsing experience" would forever change their expectations of life and give them a newfound reverence for "curated cheeses."

Jacquie listened with a pleasant smile, oohing and ahhing at the appropriate junctures. Vicar let it ride because this was meant to be a thank-you for all her work, but honestly, he was beginning to crawl out of his skin.

At the end of his five-minute-long spiel, topped by the ridiculous suggestion that they should *text* him at any time for drinks or unleavened bread, the waiter took a breath and began, "For you vegans …"

"We are not vegans," Vicar broke in starkly, spinning his index finger in a circle, suddenly not giving a shit what Jacquie's food preferences were. If she was a vegan, she could go on a dinner date with some dweeb like this, who would probably threaten to tweet human resources during his own murder.

Vicar had hoped his rudeness would encourage this gasbag to move it along, *tout suite*, but instead Pompous Hipster went on to the next item on his list, blinking and squinting spasmodically now, as if in a fugue state.

"Mmm. Mmm. Mmm. Mmm. If you have gluten intolerance …"

Vicar interrupted again, now fully annoyed. "Do you use regular water for food preparation? Because we prefer holy water."

The waiter had no quick response.

"Don't worry if you don't have a supply on hand. I'm a man of the cloth, as you can tell by my popemobile." Vicar pointed at the haloed Peugeot in the parking lot. "So just bring me a bucketful from the toilet and stand back."

The waiter rocked back on his heels for a second, shocked. "Uhhh."

"Look," Vicar levelled, "can you tell us what dishes you offer that don't require a special political allegiance or imaginary allergy?" He glared at the waiter with a piercing look, unaware of colour rising in Jacquie's face.

The waiter pointed to a section of the menu with the end of his pen and nervously said, "Here."

Vicar looked at it for all of two seconds and said, "*Pici polpette*: glorified spaghetti and meatballs. That."

Still unwilling to go off-script, the waiter asked, "Whole wheat or semolina pasta?"

Vicar looked like a serial killer about to strike.

The waiter lowered his head and said, "Riiight."

Eleven / The Moment

"Stop fooling around! You're going too fast!"

"The fastest car in the world is a borrowed one," the young man crowed with gleeful abandon. It was a beautiful, clear evening on an empty country road near the ocean. Not another car in sight and two days into a vacation. They'd had to get out of that damn house. Mother was driving him stark raving mad. They'd grabbed his dad's new SUV and taken off for a burn.

His fiancée kept screaming every time he sped up, so he made a game of it, punching the accelerator for a sharp reaction. She was slapping his arm and fairly screeching now as he thundered up the rural lane at Autobahn speeds.

As they crested the hill at an ungodly clip, a group of four deer appeared directly in front of them. The fiancée screamed. The young man slammed on the brakes and lost control as they piled head on into the cluster of animals. He tensed up as the windshield ruptured, his fiancée howled, and the vehicle rolled and began to disintegrate. Then everything was black.

▬ ▬ ▬

Driving slowly down the road back to Tyee Lagoon, Vicar turned to Jacquie in the passenger seat. "You're very quiet." She looked at him but didn't answer. "What's wrong?"

"Thanks for dinner, but that sucked."

"You didn't like your food?"

"No, I didn't like the company. You were an asshole to one and all."

Completely shocked, Vicar blurted, "What are you talking about?"

"I've never seen such rudeness in a public place, and I used to be a stripper."

He paused for a moment and flashed back on his mounting aggravation throughout the evening. Smouldering, he said quietly, "You know that some children in this world live on top of garbage dumps? Heirloom tomatoes aren't high on their priority list. Who are those people? What are they thinking of, opening a place like that twenty feet from the bush? If one of them ever got lost on the way to the shithouse, they'd end up on the menu as free-range idiot, served inside out, nestled on a bed of Vancouver Island moss." He made cougar ears with his fingers while he steered with his knees.

Before Jacquie could respond, they were confronted by an alarming sight. The entire rise ahead was a field of automobile wreckage. An explosive car accident had occurred, and parts were strewn across the road, having been thrown a great distance. An SUV was overturned, crushed, and terribly disfigured. Curving skid marks led to its large mechanical carcass in the oncoming ditch. On the opposite side of the road, at least 150 feet closer to Vicar's approaching vehicle, were the remains of a deer — possibly several deer, a shocking charnel house of them.

Judging by how it was positioned, the vehicle had not only rolled over, but might also have flipped end over end. Vicar thought he saw a deep gash where the bumper had connected with the ground and lofted the rear end high into the air. The driver must have been going at a wild speed. Deer blood, tissue, guts and imported SUV parts were everywhere. The vehicle was smoking. This must have happened mere moments ago.

Vicar sized up the situation in a glance and seized his phone. He chucked it in Jacquie's lap as he wrenched the vehicle to an emergency stop on the other shoulder and put on his flashers.

"Call 911," he said tersely, not realizing she was already on her own phone, craning her neck around to find a landmark so she could give accurate directions.

Vicar plunged through the tall meadow grass on the verge and climbed down to the SUV's driver-side window. In the dimming evening light, he saw a man and a woman upside down, hanging from their seat belts. There was blood everywhere. The airbags had gone off. The driver was motionless; his arms hung, limp, as if he was reaching toward the upturned roof.

Vicar rapped sharply on the window and yelled, "Are you all right? We're going to try to get you out. Help is on the way."

There was no response from the driver, but the passenger moved her head, which was bleeding badly; blood dripped gorily down her face into her long hair, hanging straight down like a macabre fright wig. *At least she's alive*, thought Vicar. *The driver might be out cold, or he might be a goner.*

He realized that there was no way to open the driver's door with the vehicle upside down and the door wedged shut against the dirt embankment. He raced to the other side and discovered that the passenger-side door was accessible. The window was even open a bit. He wiggled his fingers in the crack and yanked the window with all his might. With a single pull, the glass blew into dramatic shards.

He pushed his head into the vehicle. "Can you hear me? Can you speak to me?" He grabbed the hanging woman's hand and felt for a pulse. She gurgled and moaned the slightest bit. Vicar tried to open the door. It opened a mere crack, but the angle of the vehicle made this difficult; the door refused to stay open. Before he could even yell for help, Jacquie materialized before him with an old blanket in her arms.

"Help me with the door. I've got to try to get her out."

"Jesus, Tony, don't mess around. She might have a neck injury. Wait for the ambulance."

Vicar paused for the blink of an eye and thought about it. Jacquie was right. Without help, he would probably do more harm than good when he unclasped the seat belt.

He looked at her with intense concern. "How long?"

"They didn't say. Can she manage a couple more minutes?"

"I don't know. I wanna get her right side up, but if she's hurt her spine ..." An instant later came a distant siren. Some emergency responders must have been at the nearby Timmy's when the call came in.

He lunged back into the overturned truck and grabbed the dangling wrist of the driver, feeling for a pulse, looking for twitching eyelids or any sign of respiration. But he could find no signs of life. Refusing to believe what his senses were telling him, Vicar kept grasping at the man's arm in the hope that he was still alive. But still Vicar could not find a pulse. The man was not breathing. No spark, no fire. Gone.

Numb shock overcame Vicar. "He didn't make it," he called back to Jacquie. Contorting his body to the left, he looked back at her and asked urgently, "Can you see if she's breathing? I think she's still breathing."

"Yes, her chest is moving." Jacquie sounded frightened, but sharp.

In some disengaged corner of his mind, Vicar noted that she was solid, that she wasn't going to bolt. It made him feel like he could cope.

A fire truck arrived. Suddenly, there were men on the scene. Vicar crawled out of the vehicle as a fireman approached. He was white and shaking a little, but he reported, "I couldn't get a pulse from the driver, but she" — he pointed at the passenger — "is breathing."

Both victims were pulled from the wreck. The driver was laid out on a reflective blanket, his body covered from head to toe. Clearly, he was dead. The passenger lay next to the wreck on a backboard, unconscious and wearing a neck brace, two firefighter EMTs standing over her.

Vicar looked on slightly stunned, with Jacquie right by his side. She was shivering, and he began to feel chilled, too. *Slightly shocky*, he thought vaguely. He ran to his car to fetch their jackets and handed Jacquie's to her. It was some bedazzled denim effort too small to keep a Chihuahua warm. *Where the hell is the ambulance?* He glanced at her and wrapped his arms around her to give her a little warmth.

"We're losing her." There was alarm in the medic's voice. They attached an artificial respiration bag, and someone jabbed her unconscious body with a syringe.

Vicar peered up the hill, desperate to catch a glimpse of an approaching ambulance.

On the scene, there was a flurry of intense activity. The situation was dire. Vicar's vision swam a little, and he was positive that the woman was getting smaller, shrinking down to the size of a doll next to the huge men in turnout coats.

He broke away from Jacquie's wringing grip and ran to the dying woman's side. He knelt at her head, as far from the medical personnel as he could get, so he wouldn't interfere with their work. Even so, they tried to shoo him away, but he wouldn't budge.

He grasped the woman's hand and leaned down, his head lying nearly flat in the grass. He whispered into her ear, coaching her, leading her along, imploring her to keep breathing, to come toward his voice. He wouldn't let up. The rising tone of his voice conveyed his granite determination. Eventually he started getting hoarse. His mouth was dry and his hands shook, but still he beseeched her to come back, commanded her to grab the reins and ride to the other bank of the dark, churning river in which she struggled. He was Smokey Smith dragging Jimmy Tennant to safety as tracers arced just above their heads.

After long minutes, one of the medics sat back on his haunches and muttered, "I think we've lost her." The other one fell back on one arm, drained and exhausted from his efforts.

But Vicar wouldn't give up. Seeing that they had moved back, he got up on his knees and put his hand to the woman's forehead. The medics stared at him with pathos, leaving him to go through his process before stating the obvious to him, looking away in sadness and discomfort.

"You are not leaving. No! You are not fucking leaving!" Vicar made a herculean psychic effort, then punched his free hand in the grass and screamed defiantly. "*Nooo!*"

A great rasping breath came out of the formerly lifeless woman. Her eyes fluttered open. The medics looked at Vicar with utter shock for a moment, then launched back into their life-saving procedures without comment.

Meanwhile, Vicar fell backward and lay head downward in the ditch until he felt the life creeping back into him.

By the time he got back on his feet, the ambulance had arrived and loaded the woman. They were departing quickly for the hospital. One of the two medics who had been working on her strolled over to Vicar and Jacquie.

"I have never seen anything like that in my life," he said softly. He glanced at the halo on top of the Peugeot, then glanced at Vicar as if seeing the aurora borealis for the first time. Then he shook his head in wonder and departed.

Vicar and Jacquie stood there silently for a minute or two. Vicar absently toed a piece of shattered signal light that glinted on the ground in the deepening dusk. He was exhausted. Jacquie just stared up at him, her surprised eyes flicking back and forth from one of his eyes to the other. Vicar rasped a sigh, a sound as descriptive as a thousand words.

After a long, silent pause, Jacquie finally said, "I thought you were supposed to be just a drunk."

Twelve / Holy Smoke

Poutine pushed open the back door with one hand. In the other he held a large pizza box, which he plopped down on the ramshackle staff table. His sweat reeked of rotting soup mixed with a bizarre aroma from the pizza.

He carelessly thrust several telephone messages, pink paper slips of the variety that large offices had used back in the 1960s, into Vicar's hand.

"Jesus, fuck!" Poutine proclaimed coarsely. "I could eat a dead dog's ass." He opened the lid of the box.

"It smells like that's exactly what you're going to have," said Vicar, recoiling. "What in hell *is* that?" He glanced at the message slips. "And what the hell is all this?" He was genuinely puzzled.

"I dunno, but some lady's bin calling all morning. She's from the TV, dere. She wants to talk to you."

Vicar looked at him in bafflement. "What in heaven's

name do they want to talk to me about?" His forehead furrowed, and he tripped on the thought that Randy the Douche might have sicced the press on him.

"Ahhh!" Poutine exulted with great relish. "Haggis pizza from next door."

Jacquie coughed up a mouthful of tea into the sink. A moan arose from her throat.

"It's from that, uhh, Eden Burg Pizza, dere."

Edinburgh, thought Vicar, unable to decide what about this scenario should jar the most.

Poutine craned around to Jacquie, peering over his wonkily angled readers. "Whut? It's good. Have a piece. Be my guess."

Guest, guest, GUEST, Vicar's brain screamed as he shuddered at the thought of putting any of *that* into his mouth.

"I got the, uhh, deep-fried Mars Bars for dessert, dere."

Vicar and Jacquie backed out of the room as Poutine loudly licked his chops like a cartoon wolf, tucking eagerly into the dire-looking agglomeration of yuck on his brown-paper towel. "Mmm, I love *Eye*-talian food!"

Grossed out, Vicar grimaced at Jacquie, who pretended to poke her index finger down her throat, and he retreated to the shiny new phone. He cautiously dialed the number on the slip, racing through possible responses to questions he might be asked.

"Oh, hello. Are you the same Anthony Vicar who was on the scene at a car accident at Midden Hill near Tyee Lagoon last night?"

"Uhh, yeah …" he responded inelegantly. This wasn't what he'd expected at all.

"Hi, Mr. Vicar, I just wanted to confirm reports made by first responders at the scene that you brought a dead person back to life."

"Huhhh?" Mentally, Vicar began slashing through the weeds toward reality.

"A firefighter called us this morning to report the story. We were able to get three other first responders on the record, claiming almost the same thing. Do you have any comment?"

Vicar stared at Jacquie, who watched quizzically from a short distance away. "I don't even know what to say. We, that is, my friend and I" — he glanced up at her — "were first on the scene, and we just tried to help."

"The paramedics claim that they had given her up for dead, yet you somehow brought her back." A keyboard was tapping in the background.

"Why, that's insane. I just whispered in her ear to give her encouragement."

"Was she conscious at the time that you were speaking to her?"

"Nooo, I don't think so," he responded cautiously. He thought again and said more confidently, "No, she was not."

"If she was unconscious, why, then, did you think she might respond positively to you?"

"Well …" He paused, thinking back to the intense moments surrounding the action. "It seemed like they were losing her. In fact, one of them said, 'We're losing her.' I didn't think I could do any harm at that point, so I jumped in."

"What did you intend to do at that moment, Mr. Vicar?"

He paused for a long time and then said in a measured tone, "Intend? I intended to bring her back."

■ ■ ■

The crawl at the bottom of the national news the next day said, "Vancouver Island's 'Liquor Vicar' brings woman back from the dead in fatal car crash." The *National Post* had a story reporting the event under the headline, "Crash Witness Resurrects Dead Passenger." The *Globe and Mail*'s headline was, "Mouth-to-Ear Resuscitation: The Next Frontier?"

Tony Vicar started his day oblivious to all of it; the *Tyee Logger*'s front page said, "Clean Fill Wanted."

■ ■ ■

As the door swung open, Vicar was assaulted by a wall of noise emanating from a large family gathering. It set him back on his heels as the room full of partying people all noticed him at the same time and fairly screeched with excitement. For a second, he felt like a wild animal unveiled on a chat show, staring in confusion at the hubbub that met his sudden appearance. It didn't seem reasonable for his presence to extort such a response, even if he was bearing wine in the middle of the afternoon.

The hostess, a white-haired lady who strongly reminded him of Joyce Bulifant, Murray's wife on *The Mary Tyler Moore Show*, approached. Her voice was practically a *coloratura* of apology as she unleashed a torrent of the picayune upon him.

"Oh my, you're going to break your neck on that pile of shoes. Sorry about the terrible mess. Such a houseful. The last time we called you, it was a birth-dee party." She turned her back to him briefly and practically sang, "Everyone, look! It's our Liquor Vicar from the news. We have a cel-*eb*-rit-tee." There was a roar from all quarters and desultory applause.

She looked around questioningly, speaking to everyone and no one at the same time. "Was it a birth-dee or annivers-ree last time they were here?" Then, turning to Vicar: "I know we had just moved the recliner up from the basement. Jack stubbed his toe on the top stair — it sticks up a bit, and Zoey called from Regina just when it happened, and we couldn't find the phone. She's an accountant, so ..."

So? So what? Vicar very quickly realized little that was forthcoming would be germane, so he could tune in or out as he pleased. In fact, no one was paying any mind at all — likely a common occurrence. He decided to recreationally thread-along after the hostess's chatter as it careered off like a ricocheting bullet.

"Well, we were down at the shop to get the Jeep. Actually, we started down, but Jack forgot his wallet and we had to turn back. You know, it's hard to find a safe place to turn around on the highway and you might need to go quite a distance before you can manage it. Oh my, I upset my coffee on the seat and I was sopping it up with a Kleenex I had. Was it in my pocket? Or was it in my purse?" She looked around for a prompt. Finding none at hand, she continued. "One fellow beeped at us and shook his fist." She pursed her lips and theatrically shivered her shoulders in lurid recollection. "Well, Jack didn't like that at all and said, 'Up yours, buddy.'" She lowered her voice down to a mock baritone to mimic her husband's guttural rumble.

"Boy, howdy, he was hot under the collar. What were we talking about? Oh yes, the Jeep. That darn thing needed brakes *again*, and you know it costs a thousand every time you take it in, but you need good brakes in the wet. Uhh, it was raining, too — or was it snowing?"

She squinted with genuine puzzlement while attempting to recount a tale bereft of cogent arc or even any point, with the maximum number of words possible. Vicar, oddly amused, wryly gave her a title and tagline. *Joyce: Supplying Detail Without Plot Since 1950.*

A woman whom Vicar thought resembled the quintessential grand dowager, dour and scowling like a bunged-up Queen Victoria, sat in the corner, swivelling her head from the seaward window to Vicar in the open door and bellowing, "It's raining!" Vicar gazed at the vast rainforest surrounding them and suppressed a laugh.

A third lady with jet-black hair and short, severe bangs she may have sheared herself in a moment of self-loathing approached quickly and began nitpicking about the "arctic gale" howling through the open door, the mess tracked in on the mat, and an unidentified smell. "Is someone smoking? Is there a tire on fire outside?" She sniffed Vicar and asked, "Is that Hai Karate?"

Finally, she fixated on the untidy pile of shoes by the door. Vicar couldn't discern if she was deliberately trying to make him feel unwelcome, or it was just her natural talent. She got on her hands and knees, making a huge fuss about the disorderly footwear. Vicar's nearby crotch was at her eye level as her head bobbed back and forth in unintentional pantomime fellatio. Could she really be oblivious to it? Vicar tilted his head quizzically as he watched her peculiar performance.

In the distance, Dowager yelled out yet again, "It's raining!"

Some smartass in the peanut gallery sniped, "Don't pay attention, Liquor Vicar. We don't want her to come back to life."

Vicar responded with a nauseated smile.

The good lady Bulifant, oblivious to the faux blow job going on before her eyes, was still droning on about meteorological conditions during the last wine delivery. ("It might have been the one-hundred-year flood.") Bangs was organizing the shoes, inspecting the soles for mud and twigs, whispering savagely, "Dirty, filthy," and gnashing her teeth while staring holes into Vicar's pants. Dowager barked louder still: "It's raining!" As if her observation was finally going to elicit a response and, at long last, change *everything*.

Vicar snapped out of the surreality and said, "Yes, ma'am. It certainly is raining, and I've got to get back to the shop in this soup."

This jarred everyone out of their individual curious fidget spins. The Bulifantine one piped up in a dog-whistle-pitched voice, "Oooh, I'd better get you some money."

At that, Dowager barked, "Get the preacher some money!"

Vicar began to stammer a mild protest that he was named Vicar, but was not a vicar, but abandoned the attempt amid the sheer bedlam that suddenly erupted.

Bangs rose from her knees to make a big show of finding her purse. She ran a frantic search pattern of the room, bending over deeply and showing her arse square on to Vicar at least three times in twenty seconds, once even putting a knee up on the arm of the loveseat and lofting her ample posterior to previously unimaginable heights. She narrated aloud every step she took in a raspy whisper, but her purse, it seemed, was nowhere to be found. She breathily muttered that she must take her search into the bedroom — she drew out the word with brazen melodrama — pulled down her bottom lip with her index finger and disappeared. Vicar imagined her leaping off the deck to hide until the terrifying spectre of payment passed, after which she'd leap out naked from the blackberry bushes as he departed. At least she made herself scarce for the time being.

Joyce-alike had inched conversationally along from weather conditions to event type, which she now felt to a near certainty had been an "annivers-ree." She passed Vicar a wad of cash, and he quickly counted it. Dowager near the window yelped redundantly, "Get him some money!"

To Vicar's surprise, the tip was quite large, and he thanked Mistress Bulifant of the Minneapolis Slaughters sincerely as he departed. As the door swung shut he heard her say, "The last time they were here it was our annivers-ree."

The Dowager gutturally moose-called, "Did you give him some money? Millie? Millie? Did you? Did you give him? Did you? Millie? Money! Millie, Money! It's raining!"

Thirteen / The Gathering Storm

By November, the summer's verdant hues had receded, and the outdoors became something almost blue black, dark and ominous. An uninviting blanket, opaque and clammy, covered the landscape.

The deeper into the bush, the wetter and darker conditions became; mist clung to the ground like a cloud of cold discontent, and the setting sun was filtered through thick, unrelieved battleship grey. It wasn't as if it were raining — it was more like gravity had been shut off, and all moisture from heaven and earth simply floated around, a loosely packed swarm of droplets in a persistent dusk.

The dim light was so bothersome that Vicar reflexively wanted to swat at it. He shone a bright flashlight out the car window in hopes of locating the correct driveway. Sweat trickled down his back in the humidity, and the reflected glare of condensation from his window pissed him off. He growled. He imagined plunging his cold and clammy Peugeot down a tiny hidden mineshaft, never to be seen again.

As Vicar finally pulled up to the right house, through the kitchen window he saw Julie Northrop sitting at a table, sipping tea. She waved. He could see she was still wearing a neck brace all this time after the crash. He carried with him a bottle of wine hastily grabbed from a shelf at Liquor as he'd left.

He knocked politely before opening the door a crack.

Inside, he looked at Julie appraisingly, forcing himself to slow down and observe her rather than speed through pleasantries. She was drawn and vulnerable, with some slight discoloration of bruising still under her eyes almost four months later. She had suffered a dozen broken bones; her body was a fractured battlefield.

"When can you go back to school?" Vicar asked, knowing she and her fiancé had been studying in Toronto.

"I went home to Winnipeg as soon as I could travel. This is Gary's mom and dad's house. They asked me to spend some time with them if I could bear it. I might take a year off school, or maybe I'll quit. I really don't know."

Vicar glanced around the kitchen and imagined how grievously lonely it must be for all of them, here in this little house in the woods cloaked by dark clouds both real and imagined. He paused, gently gathering his words.

"I, uhhh, I am so sorry that I couldn't help Gary. He was already gone by the time I reached him." His mouth partway open, Vicar hemmed and hawed until Julie Northrop spoke.

"He died instantly, Mr. Vicar. You surely know that. I think he might have been dead before the vehicle stopped rolling. The only thing I can't understand is why I didn't die, too." Julie gazed out the window for a heartbeat and said softly, "It would have been a lot better if I had."

Vicar slowly processed her statement, his eyes glazing as he suddenly read the subtext. Anyone in her position would be fighting depression, certainly, and might even have suicidal thoughts. Her survivor's guilt might have evolved into some type of anger, perhaps toward him. Grief could overcome logic. Did she resent him for helping her, but not saving Gary? The thought dawned on him like a slow-motion punch to the gut.

"Mr. Vicar? Tony?"

He nodded and stared at her, looking right at her mouth as she spoke. The rest of the room was blurred.

"Tony, I wanted to thank you, not worry you. You did the best you could. More than anyone else could have. I can only soldier on and try to honour Gary's memory. He was going to be a great success. We were going to have a great life together," she said.

Vicar glanced down at the floor, a rusty-brown indoor/outdoor carpet that had surely complemented the avocado-green appliances a half a lifetime ago. Nervously, he began to fixate on how his underwear was bunching up, and he swivelled his hips around in the chair as if a skivvy readjustment might improve the mood. Desperate to move the conversation along, he looked up and asked cautiously, "Do you remember anything from the accident?"

Julie couldn't tilt her head back, but her eyes went toward the ceiling, and she blinked a couple of times.

"I remember telling Gary to slow down and then we hit something. I lost consciousness about then, I think."

"Is that all you can remember?"

She licked her lips and said, "I thought I was flying, like on a flying carpet. It was night and I was lost. I thought I'd lost my balance and fallen off the carpet. I was going to splat into the ground. I could hear my grandmother's voice, but I couldn't see her. She kept saying, 'Come toward my voice. You can fly, you can fly. Don't be scared, you can do it. Keep going, keep going.' Not much else, though." She lowered her head and gazed directly at him, but her eyes were distant.

Vicar stared at her with intensity. He had urged her to come to his voice. He had pushed her to keep going, going. He had been sure it was only a fluke that she'd come back from the brink. But this — this was spooky.

Fourteen / The Elephant in the Room

Poutine had supplied *gratis* all the booze for the memorial service. He was tending bar tonight in his frilly, age-yellowed tux shirt, but at the moment he was skulking around someone's donated platter of Nanaimo bars, ravenously inhaling them one after another. This past Christmas had been his best ever. Vicar's facelift of Liquor had made a huge difference, so he wanted to give back a little bit. Having just returned indoors from hoovering a fat bomber with a couple homeboys, his customary goaty aroma was muggy with an additional skunk of Texada Timewarp.

For the people he knew, his free pours were outlandishly generous. He was not fond of funerals — hated them, in fact — and simply presumed that everyone else would likewise prefer to be drunk when forced to attend one. That this one was happening after Christmas felt like a bad omen. Death was no way to kick off a new year.

He frowned as he slopped precious vodka on the counter, and he tried to locate Vicar in the gathering. He'd heard Vicar's brief account of the accident, but the story he'd heard today blew his mind. Added to that was the murmur of gossip he was overhearing at the bar.

Abruptly, Poutine set his sights on a two-tier tray filled with confetti bars — he had demolished the delectable Nanaimos, leaving behind only crumbs and an untidy smear of chocolate. Luckily, an entire banquet table was reserved for roughly two dozen different kinds of funeral squares.

In the enveloping brain fog brought on by the thunderfuck he'd just smoked, Ross Poutine daydreamed about the heretofore undiscovered similarity between bars, brownies, baked goods and ancient death symbols. Where there was a funeral, there was a scrumptious square. Would skull and crossbones go the way of the dodo, only to be replaced by depictions of chocolate nut clusters? Heavy, man. Death, traditionally to be feared, was now looking sinfully delicious. He giggled just a little too loudly and then suddenly fixated on a hole in the old Arborite counter that looked just like a tiny elephant.

■ ■ ■

Vicar stood with Jacquie over by the bingo machine, which was covered up with a grey plastic cowl.

"Gary's father was awfully brave," Jacquie said to Vicar. "I don't know how you'd find the oomph to speak at your own child's memorial service."

Vicar glanced at the father, standing with his wife in the far corner, a clutch of friends surrounding them protectively. Julie Northrop orbited wanly on the periphery.

He had been taken aback when the late Gary's father had mentioned his attempts to rescue and revive at the scene of the accident, making the whole eulogy more about Tony Vicar and his miraculous ministrations to Julie Northrop than about his dearly departed son, Gary. The tone was hyperbolic, metaphysical, even mystical — in fact, it was uncomfortably over the top. He'd missed his calling as a preacher. Over the last twenty-five years, he must have roused his customers into quite the frothy farm-implement lather while selling them tractors.

Vicar had forced himself to appear impassive throughout the entire ceremony and afterward, too, but he realized that the silly story circulating had just been confirmed by an unimpeachable source. Though the account had been rife with artistic licence and a dollop of brimstone, the attitude of the room had altered perceptibly; to his consternation, Vicar had felt his stock shoot upward.

Afterward, almost everyone had come by and gripped his hand or clapped him on the back, saying, "I just wanted to meet the miracle man," or "Good job," their dewy, saucer-like eyes showing awe. Some of them had nervously asked him to pose for a quick photo — as if he were Paul Henderson or something. Vicar had noticed Jacquie's face begin to darken as the stream of well-wishers each tried to outdo the last with superlatives, until their tone had bordered on hysterical. Vicar hadn't known how to respond. The bizarre and mysterious turn of events that had given rise to such unwarranted compliments was not digestible. He'd decided to simply leave it aside and chew on it another time.

Now, he found an old friend who wanted to talk guitars and was relieved to be briefly distracted by George Harrison's rosewood Telecaster reissue.

Catching Jacquie's eye, he panned around the room, looking at all the people present — some of them obviously talking about him in that moment — and paused to enjoy the sight of Poutine leaning over deeply, his jaw agape, profoundly stoned and drooling just a tad as he closely inspected the counter, while bemused attendees stood waiting for a drink.

Vicar flashed back on Gary's father's agonized remarks. Brought her back from death? Gave her the gift of another chance? Summoned unseen spiritual powers? Performed a miracle? *Good job?*

Fifteen / Let Them Eat Pasta

Tony Vicar stood over his sink, straining a colander full of pasta, and glanced out the window toward the country road at the end of his driveway. A microbus drove by ever so slowly, its signature heterodyning, whiny drone so distinctive that Vicar could have identified it blindfolded. He presumed it was continuing toward town.

Rinsed pasta? He'd never tried it before, but Jacquie said he was a caveman if he didn't. It made no sense, but just for fun, he'd try it this once. Why would you rinse something that had just come out of boiling water? Fussy. As the hot water drained through the colander, some splashed out of the sink and scalded his bare leg. He jumped and sloshed a puddle onto the counter. His grand plan to keep the cleanup to a minimum was going for shit.

He was cooking dinner in his tattered briefs, his usual sad evening wear. The bedraggled T-shirt he sported had been badly distorted through the years by heaven only knew what kind of torsion. The back stretched far down to almost mid-thigh, but the front rode so high that his navel was fully bared. His pits were a bit ripe, and the state of the shirt was not helped by this. But he didn't care. If some alien intelligence dropped a spaceship down into his yard, would its first judgment be about haute couture? Would it even be able to tell one human from another? Could humans tell one squirrel from another? One monitor lizard from his buddy? He managed to riff on this theme for a remarkable length of time, at one point quite grandly lecturing out loud, as if he were orating to a room filled with students.

At any rate, Vicar sometimes went to the shopping mall looking every bit as bad, but with pants, of course — he wasn't out to lunch. He felt he was making a statement with this outfit; it was his version of Einstein's go-to-hell hairdo. Somewhere in the back of his mind, he knew that when he started defending bad deportment and poor hygiene, he was off a bit.

Pasta water dripped down the cupboard door and pooled on the floor, where he was conveniently able to dab it up with his sock — but it was blazing hot. He leaned over and got the tea towel off the oven handle, chucked it down onto the puddle, and manipulated it with his foot while fooling around with the noodles.

In the background, the radio was playing some variety of dreck by a hectoring rapper back-phrasing so hard he sounded like Sammy Davis Jr. during his Nehru jacket phase. His subject matter was indecipherable, but almost certainly to do with cash and bitches. *Man, and the old folks used to think rock 'n' roll was repetitive.*

Paying more attention to the spill on the floor, Vicar fumbled the colander, and half of its contents ended up in the sink next to the pot. The rotini just lay there sadly. He grumbled and rummaged around for a big spoon. *Well, now there's a legit reason to rinse the pasta*, he thought, as he noticed the breakfast debris still covering the bottom of the sink.

As he flailed with the escaped noodles, his gloomy mind wandered aimlessly, musing randomly about things like Tamagotchis and gym memberships. By God, they were a symptom of decline. He'd read today about a health club in Vancouver that offered valet parking. Beautiful dunces with servants, same as it ever was.

In his mind's eye, he saw imperial French heads rolling around in a basket, recently separated from their noble, aristocratic bodies because they couldn't tear their focus from themselves as *tout* went to *merde royale*. Perhaps they could extinguish burning torches with seven-dollar bottles of glacier water. Or with cake made from free-range everything and a sprinkle of dust from the bones of St. Edmund, disinterred just in time to bless their multiple sets of hamstring curls, performed, of course, in front of a mirror.

Vicar could see in the dim light that the tea towel was now sopping wet, and he was only smearing the puddle around.

He felt the start of his usual slide down the all-too-familiar dark rabbit hole and tried to back away from it like a running dog trying to corner on linoleum. He decided to skip the Chianti tonight; it wouldn't help.

He poured a mountain of poorly rinsed noodles into a large bowl, the blue heavy one, now with a fresh crack heralding its imminent demise. Damn. Fave bowl — he'd gotten it at a thrift store in Victoria twenty-five years ago for about fifty cents, along with one of those sweet old railroad mugs with an image of a locomotive that said it was a 2-6-2. He didn't have the faintest clue what that meant and was loath to find out. He was aware that he had many shortcomings; he didn't want to add trainspotter to the list.

Spill ineffectively sopped up and food put on the table, he went back to the fridge to retrieve some Parmesan, his sodden left sock leaving a little trail of wet.

Then he noticed what appeared to be the same microbus passing by his house again, in the opposite direction. It crawled along, and this time he could see its occupants peering down his drive and into his window. Seeing him, a female with alabaster hair piled high pointed and turned her head toward the others. He could see flashes going off as all of them took pictures.

He drew back in surprise, not believing what his eyes were telling him. Those passengers were surveilling him, stalking him. Driving around his house to get a lookie-loo. He'd never heard of such a thing in this country, where most celebrities still mowed their own lawns.

Glancing at the street out front, he vainly attempted to find some alternative explanation, any plausible reason why they'd be out there skulking around. But there was only one: they were staking him out to get a look, like he was the real Elvis hunkered in a hotel room with tinfoil-covered windows, shacked up with Ginger and blowing holes in televisions for sport.

He'd known that memorial service was going to cause a ruckus, but this? The van came to a brief stop, and the carload of weirdos gawked for a moment, multiple phone cameras capturing the scene. Feeling rather aggravated, Vicar scrunched up his face, pulled up his shirt and stuck out his tongue. There was some excitement in the car, and then they were off.

Vicar let his T-shirt fall and stared after them, confused and feeling the unwelcome creep of something he couldn't quite see.

Sixteen / The Hinge of Fate

The lottery machine clacked out a ticket, and Poutine passed it to his customer, who had added it as an afterthought to his basket of wine.

"I sure could go for that jackpot. It's getting huge," said the customer amiably, riffling through his wallet.

"Me, too," grunted Poutine. "I'd be able to make a few altercations to my lifestyle."

The man smiled and said, "If you bless it with some good luck, maybe I'll win."

"If you want magic you'd better get *him* to bless it," Poutine said, pointing at Vicar standing over near the tequila.

"Oh, is that *him*?" The customer sounded impressed.

"Hey, Tony," Poutine called casually, "you'd better use some of your spooky stuff on this guy's ticket."

Vicar looked up from his work distractedly. "Whazzat?"

"I said, this guy needs some of your special magic on his lottery ticket, dere."

Vicar looked uncomfortable. He smiled mildly, pointed his finger like a pistol and pretended to shoot the ticket. "Bam! It's a sure winner."

The customer laughed, but soberly folded the ticket with care. "Thanks, buddy."

▬ ▬ ▬

Jacquie O stood amongst the produce clad in yoga pants and Nikes, hair under a hat, vaguely comparing cantaloupes. They looked like they'd crossed the Pacific on a raft. She glanced at the price. "Good lord, they have *got* to be kidding."

She noticed someone behind her. A woman stood there with her back to the bananas.

"Why, hello, aren't you the wife of the Liquor Vicar?"

"You mean Tony?" Jacquie responded guardedly. "Actually, we're not married."

"Mmm."

The woman looked Jacquie over as if she were some pox-ridden piece of roadkill and pursed her lips. Jacquie's tats and piercings clearly did not pass muster; ice and judgment crept over the woman's face. Inwardly, Jacquie smirked at this poor, brittle soul clearly mired in some Victorian concept of propriety. *She'd probably burst into flame if she knew I used to be a stripper.*

"Why do you ask?" Jacquie spoke the words carefully, so as not to inadvertently blurt out *piss off*.

"My husband and I are to be grandparents," the

woman announced proudly. "We hope to have an audience with him."

Eyes wide with disbelief, Jacquie asked hesitantly, "An audience with … An audience?"

"Yes, yes. We very much hope that the child will be a boy, so that the family name can continue. We feel the Liquor Vicar could assist."

Jacquie was generally quick on her feet, but right now she was at a loss. What utterly loony fantasy planet had this broad beamed in from? She glanced around, looking for cameras, or maybe some kind of unhinged Morning Zoo team camouflaged behind the romaine lettuce. But only the tiny woman stood there primly and totally straight faced, turned out in a throwback tartan getup that made her look like a walking toffee packet. She stared up at Jacquie with challenge, her lips creased firmly together in an obvious attempt to broadcast moral purity, and she was expecting an answer — one to the affirmative.

As far as she could tell, Tony Vicar couldn't consistently guide dirty dishes to the sink, so using some kinda cray-cray voodoo to select the sex of this lunatic's grandchild was likely outside his skill set. She imagined him — dressed like the King in a crown, cassock, and stick-on sideburns — giving this nutbar an "audience." What other subjects would come up? Alex Lifeson's double-necked Gibson? Sinatra's Reprise years? How it only *sounded* like Manfred Mann was singing "wrapped up like a douche"?

Jacquie bought a few seconds by gingerly putting the melons back into position and patting them deliberately, as if deeply concerned for their well-being. Finally, after a few beats of stunned silence, she replied carefully, "You'll no doubt understand that he has many demands upon his time these days. Perhaps I could take your name and number and have him respond to you at his earliest convenience."

The human shortbread tin smiled with a level of self-satisfaction that would have been infuriating, had it not been so disturbing. She proudly proclaimed, "I am Mrs. Kenneth Morrison of Sandringham Mews. Please have the Vicar call us. We are listed in the directory. Thank you and good day."

Jacquie stared after her, disbelieving and creeped out. The full-blown plaid wacko marched off quickly toward the spaghetti sauce, made a quick left, and vanished.

Seventeen / Let Us Therefore Brace Ourselves

"Oooh! You mean a private gig, like a corporate event? Did she say which band? Maybe Colony Collapse? I knew word would get out." Vicar was instantly sky high with gusto, launching into an outlandish victory celebration, half jig, half hip thrust, with a prominent overbite. He began compiling his "input list" for the event's "production manager."

Jacquie was completely bewildered. "Colony Collapse? What in the *hell* are you talking about?" she blurted, hoping her question would halt his idiotic happy dance. She'd attempted to open this discussion a few minutes earlier, and now he was failing to get the point a second time.

He looked at her smugly and replied, "New band. Farley and I only play songs by artists that have *bee* in their names, like the Bee Gees, BB King. We wanna do that King Bees song — I forget the name."

"This group exists?" she asked, knocked off balance, unable to track how the conversation had gotten here so abruptly and whether she'd be able to navigate back to the topic at hand.

"It exists on paper. I knew the idea was too awesome to stay a secret for long." Vicar softly sang "Rock Lobster" under his breath.

A secret? Ye gods. That kind of rubbish didn't need to be cloaked in secrecy. He could have screamed it from the highest mountaintop and no one would have given even the slightest shit about it. Just when she thought she understood the guy, he'd swoosh off on some night flight to rock 'n' roll heaven.

Jacquie stared down at the floor for a few moments and distracted herself with the pattern on the kitchen tile — a sliver of late afternoon sun glowed upon it.

As he fiddled with the stereo, Vicar erupted in atonal song. "Daydream BEE-liever and a homecoming queen … bee …" He smirked.

Jesus, I think his landing strip has a few potholes that need paving, Jacquie thought, aggravated by his lack of concern. The disconnect she was witnessing made her short of breath. Usually, Vicar seemed so normal — bright, even — but mention one of his bands, and he was off like a terrier after a rodent. She flashed on a memory of her auntie, a schoolteacher with an advanced degree in education, who, with a straight face, had once told her about a *friend of a friend* who had come home from Hawaii with a pimple that later erupted and spewed forth a thousand baby spiders.

Feeling the urgency of the situation boiling up, Jacquie looked up and sharply said, "Tony! Hey!" She clapped her hands. Vicar stopped singing and looked at her. "She wants an *audience*. You know, like you're the pope or something."

Vicar levelled his gaze at her for a heartbeat or two, then laughed. "Oh, piss off!" He began humming again.

Even with three years of psych under her belt, Jacquie couldn't figure out if this music thing was enthusiasm, denial, or a mental disorder.

"Tony, she wants you to use your hidden powers to choose the sex of her grandchild."

Vicar tilted his head, his face screwed tight in disbelief, as if he were seeing through a silly little prank.

"I am not kidding. You must believe me. She is loony. She asked — she practically demanded an audience. This is scary." She paused for a moment. "You have to be careful. This is beginning to get out of hand."

Seeing the grave look on her face, Vicar stiffened, the cloud-cuckoo talk of his band vanishing like smoke.

▪ ▪ ▪

The BC Lottery Corporation's press conference was under way in a brightly lit, glass-walled media room in Richmond, across the bridge from Vancouver.

"Well, actually, I bought it at the liquor store in Tyee Lagoon, at the same shop where that Liquor Vicar works." There was a buzz from the small crowd of enthusiasts and press. Everyone had heard that news story. Cameras zoomed closer.

"Is he the person who sold this five-million-dollar winner to you?"

The man thought for a second and then said, "Actually, no, but when we asked him to bless the ticket for good luck, he did, and, it worked!"

"Really? He blessed the winning ticket?"

He held the mic steady but looked all around the room to elicit a response, which he duly succeeded in doing. "Yeah, he told me it was a 'sure winner.'"

The media started writing their story before they'd even left the room.

Eighteen / There Are No Small Gigs

The red Peugeot rattled down the road, laden with guitars, speakers, and a breathless Jacquie O. She was in the front seat, twisted uncomfortably, her high heels stuck to the floor mat with carelessly spilled root beer. A long microphone stand was poised to take out her eye, and she held a milk crate full of foot pedals on her lap.

How had all this come about? One moment she'd been looking up a recipe online, and the next, she was rushing out the door to go with Vicar and his buddy Farley Rea to the Tyee Trapper.

"I think those guys missed the ferry."

"What guys?" she asked.

"The group they booked from Vancouver — Old Man Smell."

Jacquie rolled her eyes. "Riiight. How could I forget? Remind me who they are?"

Vicar replied sonorously, "They are a really good vocal band. They do a ton of Crosby, Stills & Nash. I think they're better than Marrakesh Espresso from Seattle."

"Mm-hmm," Jacquie said noncommittally. This insider stuff was proving too much to track. They got so precious about it. She sometimes felt like a bowling groupie hanging around with polyester nerds who never stopped talking about wrist supports. Lord, if she got herself a polka-dot skirt, she could load up a basket full of bratwurst and break hearts down at the lanes.

She looked over her shoulder at Farley sandwiched between an amplifier and an ancient suitcase full of cables. He wore an orange toque pulled so low he looked like a troglodyte, with bold stitching on it spelling out the word *MEAT*. A poor fashion choice, it did nothing to make him look more intelligent. He wore antique Dacron flares in a bold check too ghastly for public use. Also, high-top moccasins with rabbit-fur pompoms. Jacquie's flesh crawled at the sight of them. But he blushed as he grinned at Jacquie. He seemed extremely nervous in her presence.

He followed Vicar around like a puppy, and every once in a while, he did something hilarious. Jacquie supposed that was why Farley was there. The pompoms must be part of his mascot's costume. As silly as he looked, she saw the puppy love in his eyes and felt warmth for him. He reminded her of junior high school.

Vicar and Farley had rushed to get organized and set up, having only an hour's notice. At the stroke of 8:00 p.m., Vicar got on the microphone.

"Good evening. We're the Loitering Goitres, here for your listening pleasure."

Hearing this, Jacquie squinted uncomfortably. Vicar's tired patter reminded her of the blowhard DJs at her old club, Beaver Fever — they'd all sounded like game show hosts on cough medicine.

Vicar and Farley commenced their first song, and Jacquie was immediately concerned. Somebody was badly out of tune. She presumed it was Farley, because Vicar kept looking at him with annoyance. Whoever the offender was, the music sounded awful. Farley was unaware, dancing about without a care and making his pompoms bounce merrily. She tried to look away but couldn't.

The song seemed to match the era of Farley's *Hawaii '76* T-shirt. It left her totally cold. It was a grandpa song, super boring, painful, like music from *The Love Boat*. Plus, Vicar was constantly fiddling around with the many gadgets he'd set up and never looked up at the small crowd. *Why, oh, why have they never rocketed to stardom?* she thought wryly, then quickly rebuked herself for the cynicism. Vicar was acting like this was Carnegie Hall. Farley was sweet and adorable and completely out to lunch.

Jacquie tried to put critical thoughts out of her head — she knew Vicar loved this, even though he wasn't nearly as good as he thought he was. What harm could come of it? Her own father had strummed a little guitar. Yet Vicar took it so damned seriously. She had known some dancers like that — still holding on to the dream late into their forties, threadbare exotic grannies.

The Trapper was almost empty. To buy time for Farley's inept approximation of retuning, Vicar got on the mic. "Thanks, folks. If you have any requests, just bring 'em up — written on a twenty-dollar bill."

He introduced Farley and then himself. There was a sudden hum of recognition from the audience. Instantly, all ten audience members were on their phones texting furiously.

By the beginning of the second set an hour later, the place was nearly full.

Vicar leaned over to Farley and quietly said, "Let's give 'em 'Radar Love.'"

Farley, now wearing a glow-in-the-dark necklace and some random chick's cat's-eye sunglasses, had just come indoors after the break, overwhelmingly stoned. He gazed absently into the distance. "How does that one go again?"

Vicar laughed, at first thinking he was taking the piss, but soon saw the slightly ashen look on Farley's face.

"You gotta be kidding me. A Labrador Retriever could play that bass part." Vicar grabbed his guitar neck and started quietly playing the bass line, singing along with it. "Dum, dum, dum, dum, dum, dum, nn-dah-dah!"

Farley looked at him. "Oh, man," he croaked.

Vicar was furious. This might be an unadvertised last-minute-fill-in show in the distant boondocks, but the place was packed, and they simply had to nail it.

"Farley, goddamn it, if you fuck this one up ..." he said, glaring.

Again, Farley croaked. "Oh, man."

Vicar frowned and started the riff. He went round and round about eight times before Farley fell in, but at least he had it when he entered. At the top of the second verse, Farley stumbled a bit and never really regained his composure. He began thrashing around on the neck, sliding like a duck landing on a frozen lake. *Basso glissandos* erupted like geysers in lieu of the intended part. By the big section in the middle, there was no similarity between what the two men were playing. It was a complete train wreck. Livid, Vicar ended the song as quickly as he could.

He extended his arm toward Farley and said, with deliberate intent, "Oh my, oh my, ladies and gentlemen! On bass guitar, Farley Connor Rea. Yes, *Connor Rea*. You heard right, folks. Cruel, cruel parents. *Connor-Ree-Ya*. Sympathize with the poor devil after the show."

Farley looked at his feet, moaning, "Oh, man."

Vicar was distracted by the sight of the audience on their feet and slowly flowing toward the stage. Bewildered, he started another song, forgetting to first tell Farley which one it was.

The instant the song became recognizable to the crowd, screams of approval took him aback. He grinned and started rocking with all his heart.

Once again, Farley totally screwed the pooch, doing an about-face and pretending to turn knobs on his amp — as if the amp were making the mistakes. For a while, he ceased playing and just nodded in time like a bobblehead doll.

Vicar was perplexed. Music, he zealously believed, carried a deep meaning, if delivered with precision. The part he had never quite apprehended was that it became invisible if delivered with precision only. Farley was completely out of it and ruining the whole show. Yet the audience loved everything, every wrong note, every blooper, every forgotten part, every stupid leap and jump. It was like the Elvis schtick, but even more intense. And so, Vicar just forged on ahead, with or without poor Farley. The room was well onside. Vicar had never felt this kind of response before. Karma was repaying him for the three weeks he'd spent learning the chords to that damn Steely Dan song!

Suddenly Vicar was Bono. Inspired, he wanked at his guitar in a ham-handed attempt to ad lib a solo, grimacing with the standard-issue rock orgasm face and thrusting his guitar theatrically like a prop penis. A string snapped and began waving around like an errant eyebrow hair, rendering his solo attempt — already at the limits of his abilities — impossible. A little too excited, he accidentally stepped on his cable and briefly unplugged himself. Nevertheless, the audience roared its approval. One tall, shapely girl with luxuriant red hair down her back, an absolute goddess, licked her lips seductively. *Wow!*

He was only dimly aware of Jacquie sitting at the back of the room, watching the strange turn of events with a look of disbelief.

Nineteen / Rack and Pinion

A crowd of people walked into Liquor, all grinning like they had something exciting to share. Vicar didn't recognize any of them and certainly didn't have a clue what all the smiling was about. The man in the lead had a full posse in tow, and one of them had a huge camera hanging around his neck. Vicar felt his creaky mental Rolodex spinning and suddenly realized the lead guy was the man who'd won the lottery the other day. He'd bought the ticket here, from Ross Poutine.

"Hi there, Vicar!" he exclaimed, a little too loudly for a personal greeting in an otherwise deserted shop.

Vicar could piece together that something was afoot. He presumed the man was here to thank Poutine for selling him the big winning ticket. "Ross isn't here," he blurted with concern. "He won't be back till tomorrow morning."

"Oh, don't worry. I've come to see *you*."

Vicar phased into the middle distance and tried to imagine why.

"It was your special blessing that gave me the luck. So here is a little thank you." The man handed Vicar an envelope.

A thank-you card. Well, that's nice. "Thanks!" said Vicar, genuinely touched. "What are you going to do with your winnings?"

"Oh, pay off the house. Maybe buy another one and rent it out. Travel a little. Caroline wants to go to Africa." He smiled at his wife, who stood near him.

"Mmm, Africa, that sounds fantastic." Vicar imagined how cool it would be to see the wildlife in person.

"We can afford to do a few other things, too." There was a brief pause, and the man held out his hand. "I don't think we ever officially met. I'm Barry."

"Nice to meet you, Barry. I'm Tony."

"Oh, yes, I know who you are." Another pregnant pause, then Barry urged, "Open it up." The camera came up, and Barry's wife sidled up to him and grabbed his hand.

Vicar opened the envelope. As expected, it was a lavish thank-you card. He dutifully read it, hiding his dislike of factory poetry, but suddenly, from within its folds popped out a cheque. It was made out to Tony Vicar in the amount of fifty thousand dollars.

For a moment, Vicar gaped at it, slack jawed, and then lost his grip on it. The cheque fluttered to the floor and Vicar, momentarily stunned, couldn't decide whether to pick it up or to say something. He did neither. He simply stood there in shock as the camera flashed again and again and the couple howled with delight.

Finally, he found his voice. "Wh-wh-what? Whyyy?" he croaked. "Why are you giving me this?"

Barry smiled brightly at his wife, cocked his right hand into a finger pistol, and said, "Bam! Right back at-cha! 'Member? You blessed my ticket. You told me it was a sure winner, and it *was*! This was the least we could do to thank you."

Vicar stood there, completely dumbstruck.

— — —

"No, you are not hearing things. I said a cheque for fifty thousand dollars. No, no, not fifteen. Fifty. Five-zero *thousand*. I'm not screwing with you, Jacquie. I'm holding the damn thing in my hands. What do I do?"

Vicar was flapping around the store like a headless fowl, half excited, half panicked. He kept thinking about the clutch on his Peugeot. He could afford the repair now.

Just as suddenly, he swerved and began to tell himself that this was ludicrous. He hadn't done anything. He couldn't accept this gift; it was insane. Then he thought about that goddamn Visa bill that had shackled him into penury for the last five years — it could be a distant memory with one mouse click. Surely there'd be enough dough left over for a guitar — maybe the '60 Les Paul he'd been drooling over on eBay.

"Hold tight," Jacquie said forcefully. "Don't do anything. Just close the shop, shut off the lights, and have a glass of wine. I'll be there in fifteen minutes."

— — —

Her laundry-folding abandoned, Jacquie practically hurled the phone across the room onto the soft couch and hopped on one foot while pulling a shoe on the other and scanning the room for her purse. She had to get there before he started buying more damned guitars. Within thirty seconds she was in her car, reversing out of the driveway like a rail-mounted missile.

Two days later, as Poutine manoeuvred the rumbling Chevelle into its usual stall, he saw a gang of people scuffling around the parking lot, a couple of them holding signs or placards. Election? No, there was no election coming up that he knew about. What were they up to? One of them was photographing his store. Instantly, his back went up. *What the hell is going on here?*

The photographer leaned down to the boulevard and yanked out a handful of bedraggled grass long out of season. Confused, Poutine looked again at the signs. One of them, handwritten in thick marker, said, *Bless My Ticket Vicar.*

Poutine got out and stood beside his car, staring angrily at them, not at all sure what to do. One member of the group, a tall, curvaceous beauty with long jet-black hair, looked back at him with challenge, raised her shirt, and stuck out her tongue. The rest of them took her lead and did the same.

"Whoa, man," exclaimed Poutine, "that is one helluva rack."

Twenty / Van Damage

Vicar got wind of the impending closure of the town's ancient hotel, the Agincourt, via gossip. He daydreamed about buying that old junk heap, gutting it, and dressing it up. He remembered once having gone in there with someone — his mother? *Man, she's been gone a long time now*, he mused. He recalled the terrible condition of the red carpet in the entryway. The old loggers would stomp out their smouldering butts on the rug just before going in. Cigarettes. What a beastly habit.

This was all vacationland now — a guy could be the innkeeper of cool boutique digs if he had a budget to work with. Vicar's imagination ran wild at the thought of what he could create out of that beat-up old saloon. Back when he was a kid, everyone had simply called it the beer parlour, and even then, only itinerant loggers had ever stayed in the hotel rooms. It was the only place in town, and it had a salty reputation. He'd thought it was called the "Asian Cord," as in a *cord* of wood, until he was older, never having given much thought to the writing on the sign. It was a no-star hotel where drunken bulldozer drivers peed in the sink at night rather than walk down the hall to the shared toilet.

But its coffee shop had been famous for its fabulous pies, displayed on a revolving wire rack. He remembered the tub-shaped soda fountains that circulated Orange Crush, his favourite, in a tantalizing show. The interior was painted a disquieting mint green, but at the time, he'd loved it. All the kids would stare in the windows as they walked by.

On the south corner was the beer parlour, which had used to be *For Men Only*. It had a long bar made of locally harvested lumber — fir, most likely — lovingly built by hand long before the days of such luxuries as power sanders and routers. Every joint had been crafted by some guy with a chisel, a sharp eye, and a steady hand. Whoever he was, here's hoping he'd gotten the very first pint ever poured there.

Vicar had once snuck in underage. He remembered having a draft at that old bar, out of a tapered glass that featured an imperial crown and a white plimsol line. The brass foot rail had been grimy, and the face of the bar down near the floor was scarred by thousands of boots. They'd eventually torn out that old beauty, for some inexplicable reason, and replaced it with a more modern, unlovely horror of neon and steel.

Vicar had always had a romantic notion about being a barman. Not some airborne-mug-dodging saloon keeper, but a true barman in the civilized tradition — the kind of barman who was loved by all and would fill every regular's order from memory as soon as they set foot upon the premises, ready to slide the correct pint neatly into their outstretched hand when they approached the bar. What a gesture of respect. What a feeling of comfort and reward to the customer. Do that for a man once, and he'd come back a thousand times.

If only he could create a pub with a homey feel, where everyone would truly want to go; warm and welcoming, a safe, womb-like haven. No fights. No glass or potted palms. Dark wood, nooks and cozies, pictures of our heroes, maybe: a shadow box containing their medals or trophies or diplomas or photos in which they held up a gargantuan salmon. No shit beer, only heavenly nectar selected with care, with no allowance given to the shortcuts of economy.

After five minutes of dreaming, Vicar deliberately dropped the subject. The fifty thousand he suddenly found himself with wouldn't even be enough for a down payment. The land alone — yikes! Nothing shy of a miracle would allow that dream to come true.

■ ■ ■

It was bucketing down, as usual, but Vicar enjoyed leaving a movie theatre on a rainy night.

"What did you think?" Jacquie asked Vicar.

"I think that if you installed a device on her mouth that filtered out whinging, no sound would have come out of her at all."

"Ahh, so you loved it," she replied dryly.

"Sorry, Jack. I just never had much patience for rom-coms. So forced. Unrealistic. Do women actually fantasize about scenarios like that?"

She glanced at him. "Well, in a way, yes. At least it's better than those things men watch. Judo-chopping jet planes and kicking Jeeps. Double the Van Damage — you know, so violent. Infantile. Rom-coms may not be your cup of tea, but at least they're feasible."

"Right, well, my fantasies are somewhat different …" He leered cartoonishly at her cleavage.

"Oh, you caveman!"

She laughed and playfully slapped his arm. Vicar trusted that she knew he was joking. He was always gentlemanly to her, in his own rustic way. Anyway, few men could stand movies like that. Even the guys in the cast had probably been retching during filming.

"I put that cheque in the bank," he said.

"I hope you're going to do something with it other than pay bills."

He chuckled. "Oh, yes, my dear. I put it in my savings account, where it will gain one percent per annum, and I will be a millionaire around the time our robot overlords take control of the planet."

"Mmm," Jacquie agreed. "Money's not worth what it used to be anymore."

Vicar turned to her and smirked. She was much younger than he. If she only knew.

They drove in silence until they rolled up to Vicar's house. He parked right next to her car.

"You're coming in, right? Nightcap?"

She pretended to be coy. "I suppose I could have a cup of tea."

"Do you wanna have a sleepover?" he asked boyishly. "I have popcorn."

She cackled and opened the car door.

Vicar led the way to the house and stopped short in front of the door. It was slightly ajar. "I'm sure I locked the door before we left."

Jacquie squinted. "I can't recall."

Vicar raced back through his recollection of their departure. He'd been talking to Jacquie, who, if he remembered correctly, had been putting on lip goo. He must have gotten sidetracked and left without locking the deadbolt. Also, the doorknob was sometimes a bit balky.

He entered, and upon finding the house completely undisturbed, blew off his concerns. He just wanted to get his coat off and fire up some snacks.

Jacquie kicked off her shoes and flopped down on the couch theatrically; a huge cloud of dust billowed out in response. She grimaced and put her hand over her nose and mouth.

"Good lord, Tony. Don't you have a vacuum cleaner?"

"It wouldn't be so bad if you didn't body-slam it," he retorted over his shoulder as he turned the corner to his bedroom.

"Well, you can certainly afford a fancy vacuum now," she quipped.

Vicar was met by a dark figure standing two feet in front of him. He was so frightened that he yelped, jumped back violently, lost his footing on the slippery hall runner, and fell backward onto the floor. He cracked the back of his head on the tile and lay there, disoriented and moaning.

Jacquie leaped up. "Tony? Are you all right?" She saw him lying dazed on the floor and dashed over. "Oh, my God!" She ran her hand down the wall to the light switch and flicked it on. There before them stood a woman clad only in black stockings, a garter belt, and high-heeled shoes. Jacquie let out a terrified shriek. "Who are you?" she screamed.

The nearly nude woman, totally unabashed, provocatively slid one arm up the door jamb, looked icily at Jacquie, and replied, "Who are *you*?"

Jacquie turned to Vicar, still incapacitated on the floor, and demanded accusingly, "Who is *she*?"

Walleyed, his bell still ringing, he gargled something unintelligible.

Jacquie rounded on the woman again, incensed. "You get the hell out of here!" she yelled.

The woman just sneered. "The Vicar is mine."

Now Jacquie snapped back to Vicar. "How long has this been going on?" She was suddenly a dangerous wounded animal.

Now beginning to gather himself, Vicar addressed the nude invader. "Who *are* you?"

Jacquie climbed over Vicar's supine body, screamed, and launched herself at the naked siren, her fists flailing. The woman fell back against the wall, and Jacquie tripped over Vicar's legs. She went down, and the intruder leaped cleanly over Vicar. A split second later, Jacquie was in pursuit, springing onto the intruder's back.

Vicar hefted himself up on one elbow and watched the tackle in fascinated horror. He winced as Jacquie shoved the intruder into the potted plant that she'd insisted his house needed. He'd told her he didn't want any damn plants in his house, but he couldn't have foreseen this reason. The terracotta pot plunged into one of his beautiful studio monitors. The speaker crashed down into an unceremonious heap with an eruption of potting soil, ceramic, and metal, the woofer fairly exploding out of the cabinet. The entire corner of his living room was torn asunder, decorated with randomly scattered spears of mother-in-law's tongue.

Jacquie slowly got up, only to duck as the woman fired a high heel at her from close range. It arced over Jacquie's lowered head and nailed Vicar right in the gut. He grunted, glad it hadn't hit him a few inches lower. He couldn't imagine having to explain to the ER doc that his jewels had taken a death blow from a hurtling fuck-me shoe during a home invasion by a naked woman. They'd have put him in a rubber room.

Now both were standing, grappling for advantage. This dangerous unidentified woman had height on little Jacquie and twisted her over hard, but Jacquie wasn't about to go down without her pound of flesh. She brought her knee up into the stomach of the exposed woman while viciously yarding on her short, spiky hair, and they both fell, taking Vicar's Martin D-35 down with them, blasting the guitar to flinders in the process. Then an entire wall unit collapsed, burying them in a heap of fossils and tchotchkes. A Texas mickey weighing at least sixty pounds and filled with twenty years' worth of pocket change narrowly missed Jacquie's head and detonated in a frightening starburst of silvery shrapnel. Amid the utter destruction and chaos, Vicar began to appreciate the main theme of this bizarre scenario. Before him was a no-holds-barred, full-on wrestling match between two women who were, from what he could tell, fighting over *him*. This was most assuredly a first.

Jacquie laid such a licking on the interloper that she was soon sprawled, starkers and unconscious, on the living room floor, covered in glass, nickels and dimes, and one ironically positioned Barenaked Ladies CD. Vicar retrieved the CD from its resting place, took a prolonged gander — which elicited a growl from Jacquie — and then covered the woman in a blanket.

■ ■ ■

Within a couple of minutes of her arrival, Con-Con was piecing together the fantastic tale. Eyes wide, she was doing her level best to stay professional. As she assessed the undeniable evidence of a shocking amount of violence, she wanted to double over in laughter at what would have been a bizarre happening even in San Francisco's Tenderloin. Here in Tyee Lagoon, the incident was as hard to believe as a Sasquatch driving an Uber.

Con-Con got the strange woman up off the floor and put her in the back of the cruiser, wrapped in a blanket. She was holding a Kleenex to her profusely bleeding nose, and her stockings were a torn-up disaster. Con-Con got an eyeful of the goods as she manoeuvred herself into the car. *What a treacherous, blazing-hot mess*, she thought.

She took Jacquie's statement, talking with her quietly, calming her down, and getting her an ice pack for the growing shiner under her eye. Jacquie was bashed up pretty good, but she'd apparently knocked this devious Amazon for six. Vicar's little cottage was a complete ruin. He muscled an overturned chair back to its feet, collapsed into it, and surveyed the carnage.

At the entryway, Con-Con said, "I think I've got the picture, Jacquie. I have to ask Tony for a statement, too. This is one of the weirdest calls I've ever made." In low tones, she muttered, "I gotta admit, though, she has one helluva rack."

Twenty-One / Goodbye Yellow Brick Road

Serena was tall and shapely, with a classic figure like Anita Ekberg. Her ample, high bosom was lavishly displayed and magnetic to the eye. Her posture was stately when she was of a mind to play that role, and her look was imperious, devastating, or come hither, depending on her rapidly vacillating moods. In a tank top, she elicited wolf whistles; in a cocktail dress, she stopped a room cold. She could be icy or intimidating or dripping with sweaty animal heat. Even with a broken nose, she was stunning.

While she spent the night in detention, the Mounties treated her like a movie star who'd gotten a parking ticket. And when her minions bailed her out next morning, the two cops on duty bade her a cheery farewell, both grinning like schoolboys.

Serena's gang were more flunkies than companions. All male, all maintaining that they were just her friends while hiding their erections, every one of them slavish, hovering around hopefully.

She sashayed to the microbus, uncaring of the chaos she'd created — bent, in fact, on producing more. She vowed to avenge last night's insult and to bag the Vicar, to boot. She was not accustomed to being refused, let alone to harsh rebuke of the sort that little bitch had doled out. She would pay severely; Serena would have her revenge and her deeply satisfying reward. The Vicar was hers — she would be his consort. *Perhaps this one will guide me*, she thought.

"Hey, Serena, whaddya gonna do to her?"

This from Andy, the yappy one who was constantly trying to insert himself into the centre of events.

"It's going to be worse than what I did to that investment banker in the Maserati."

They all laughed in cruel agreement, but even the coldest of them also shuddered at the thought of the unspeakable damage her sharp teeth had done during that awkward front-seat tryst. Ghastly, just ghastly. More than anything, Serena was crazy. Those eyes, those spinning wild eyes. You could practically see Mel Brooks falling into their counter-rotating spirals. Considering the high anxiety her presence invariably induced, that seemed only right.

She had no idea why, but she just knew she was a chosen one. She was sure she had been born great, and she was waiting impatiently for everyone else to notice. Heaven help the person who stood in her path.

She was known for inexplicable tangents, visionary "missions" that few others would have recognized as anything but lunacy. However, she worked them as if they were critical acts in an epic tale of her ascendance to great heights, from where she would survey her kingdom while her followers recounted her story again and again. Her little altar boys could practically feel truth unravel as she cunningly manipulated random events and moulded them to suit her own narrative. She specialized in seeking out the suggestible.

The more reckless the exploit, the better, but her antics mostly just added to her criminal record: breaking and entering, stalking, petty theft, assault, vandalism. She spray-painted ghastly statements on any flat surface; incited violence in crowds, even at shrubby folk fests; and performed a catalogue of crazy stunts based on her twisted sense of what she called her "destiny" and the intricate fantasy that was her inner life. She had quite a pile of restraining orders for a woman of only twenty. To her, they were a bit of a status symbol, like medals to a soldier. She instinctively knew how to use her beauty to nefarious advantage.

"Turn right here, Jeet," she commanded. "Stop at a mall. I need ice for my face and some makeup. And step on it. We don't have all day."

She had the looks of a movie star, but the instability and explosiveness of uranium. She had been neglected and abused as a child; now she left a chaotic trail of scarred and broken men — and a few women — in her wake.

Twenty-Two / No Garden-Variety Johnson

Jacquie O's shiner was more than a mouse under her eye; it was a huge swamp rat. The bridge of her nose was split and bloody; both eyes were badly blackened, the right one swollen shut and covered with gauze; and there were scratches all over her face and neck. She wore huge sunglasses sparkling with rhinestones, each lens nearly the size of a side plate, that made her look like Elton John as seen through an aquarium. They were the biggest sunglasses she had in her dresser. A hoodie over her head concealed her face from all but direct examination.

She followed Vicar into Liquor. Poutine took one look at her and blurted, "What does the other guy look like?"

"*She*," Jacquie grumbled. "She looks a lot worse, and so she should."

Poutine's eyes bulged, and he silently looked to Vicar for explanation.

Vicar just shrugged tiredly and whispered, "I'll explain later."

Head down, with the flat of her hand visoring her face, Jacquie mumbled, "Ross, can I just go back and make myself a cup of tea?"

Poutine practically fell over himself escorting her to the staff room with obvious concern. Sometimes that fusty old goat was a real softie.

He ran over to the store to get her the tea she liked and a couple of lemons. In a club-footed attempt to give comfort, he also grabbed a cellophane bag filled with mass-produced mini donuts from a clearance bin, oblivious to the fact that stale baked goods discovered in a forlorn crate didn't quite fit the brief as comfort food for the discerning diner, or even the undiscerning one.

Back at Liquor, an off-duty Con-Con popped in to buy some chardonnay for her mother. When she heard that Jacquie was in the staff room, she strolled in back and sat down. Vicar ambled over, too, and the three of them recounted the bizarre details of the truly crazy night they'd had.

"I was so surprised, I nearly crapped my drawers!" Vicar exclaimed.

Laughing, Con-Con agreed. "No doubt. I can't imagine how I'd react to that situation." She winked. Jacquie, who was eager for a change of mood, cracked up loudly. Con-Con's partner was named Nancy and they had been together for years.

"Yeah, well, uh, I did notice she had one helluva rack," Vicar said.

Jacquie and Con-Con both cranked their heads hard toward him, feigning shock. Jacquie, her one good eye glaring balefully, exclaimed, "Why, you sexist bastard." Vicar was brought up short and retreated in confusion. As he left they began to cackle mischievously.

■ ■ ■

The afternoon was very slow, and so Poutine clumsily attempted to chat about music. It was a subject about which he knew nothing, while Vicar, of course, was sure he knew most everything. The last recording Poutine had purchased was *Highway 61 Revisited* by Bob Dylan, likely in the week it was released. This was to say, on vinyl, in the previous century, back when *Bonanza* had been the toast of prime-time TV and Captain Kirk was still enrolled in flight school. Poutine no longer had a turntable, and his Chevelle was stock, featuring a wretched-sounding AM radio in the dash that still vainly searched, Vicar was convinced, for a Petula Clark song to play.

"Y'know, they say Bob Dylan's got that, uhh, perfect pitch, dere ..." Poutine gave Vicar a lofty look. Vicar smirked and quickly swallowed his coffee so he wouldn't spew it out. "Whut? Whut? That's what I heard," Poutine backpedalled.

Too precious about music to simply appreciate his employer's attempt at amiable chatter, Vicar responded, "Yes, also Ernest Borgnine. And Triumph the Insult Comic Dog. Oh yeah, and Scooby-Doo."

Poutine departed, grumbling, and Vicar continued to snicker until the phone rang. It was Con-Con calling from the police detachment. Vicar tensed; he knew that he might still be charged for assaulting Randy the Dickhead, and he'd been worriedly awaiting the pronouncement.

"I just wanted to inform you that we won't be moving ahead with charges against you. Our investigation has revealed that Mr. Johnson had assaulted his partner earlier that day, and he has a sufficiently long record of domestic violence and other assaults that we feel you acted in self-defence, as you have asserted. As far as we are concerned, it's a closed matter."

Vicar took a long, relieved breath. "Thank you."

"You're welcome, Tony."

"Seriously, though … is his name really Randy Johnson?"

There was silence at the other end for a moment, then Con-Con let out a loud snort.

The show is standing room only. He floats above the audience, observing them. The stadium is massive. He suddenly finds himself on deck, side stage, but he can't get to his position. His feet are stuck to the floor. Someone slings a guitar over his shoulder. Oh no, it is a left-handed guitar — he has no idea how to play it! The song begins. He tries to play chords with the wrong hand but can't do it. A spotlight lights him up brilliantly, and he realizes then that he has no clothes on …

Vicar awoke with a start and glanced over to his left, where Jacquie lay sleeping. He hoped to just lie in for a few minutes. Once Jacquie was up, there would be no avoiding the day, but until then, he could cheat a little. He winced when his stomach gurgled loudly, as though it had just said, "Bryan."

Feeling nature's call, he gingerly slid out of bed, taking every caution not to wake Jacquie. She was on her side, facing away from him. If he did this correctly, he'd be able to get back in bed and sleep a little longer, maybe get to the bottom of that silly dream. To his surprise, he managed to thread the needle: he didn't wake her, and he avoided that noisy floorboard that also seemed to say "Bryan" when you stepped on it. It struck him that he had once hiked past a sheep that had similarly seemed to call out that name, and he tried to put it all together. *Were those funny mushrooms on the pizza last night? Oy.*

In nothing but a ghastly pair of tighty-whities with a blown-out arse — just like every other pair of underwear he owned — Vicar silently padded toward the bathroom, noticing that they had forgotten to close the curtains before they went to sleep last night. Happily, light was streaming in; the morning was bright and clear. He brushed by the end table and knocked a magazine onto the floor, then bent over deeply to pick it up, in the process stretching taut his regrettable underwear and baring most of his glaringly untanned bum.

There was a loud hail and cheer from the outdoors. Badly startled, Vicar shot up and looked behind him, through the window. To his utter shock, the front lawn was crowded with people sitting cross-legged, many of them now rising to their feet in an ovation, a greeting better suited to a conquering hero. Dozens of strangers were gathered on his front lawn, apparently just dying to say hello. Some sat in the lotus position like a scene cut and pasted from a Summer of Love flashback. Realizing the state of his undress and his recent Freddie Mercury–style genuflection, Vicar shrieked a little and fell to the floor in mortification, then panther-crawled back to Jacquie and safety, as if someone had lobbed a grenade.

Racing on hands and knees to the bedside, he grabbed Jacquie and shook her in a panic.

"Jack, Jack … people." He was at a loss for words.

She rolled over and grunted, "Huh?"

"People. There." He grunted and gestured at the window like a startled Neanderthal.

Jacquie blinked a couple of times and attempted to size up the situation. Half awake and half mocking, she pointed at the window and said, "People?"

"People." His eyes were rimmed with alarm.

Amused, Jacquie rolled out of bed clad in Vicar's only remaining clean T-shirt, pulled apart the slats of the blinds, and peered out. Then she shrieked.

Ross Poutine pulled a cupped hand full of loonies and toonies out of his pocket and dumped the coins onto the bar table in a loud cascade.

"Looks like about twenny-fie bucks, dere … We can hava coupla beers."

Vicar looked at the coinage. "Uh, okay. But I have to drive. Not too much."

Poutine growled, but assented.

"So, what the hell happened?" he asked once they'd gotten their drinks.

Vicar paused and collected his thoughts. "I'll be goddamned if I know, Ross. We came home from the movie and she was just there, naked as a jaybird, waiting for me in the dark. Jacquie flipped and beat the living hell out of her."

Poutine smiled tightly and looked down at the floor. "That's m'girl …"

"Well, yeah. She's no pushover, but God almighty, what a horrible scene. Total destruction of my little house!"

Vicar wasn't delighted about the violent antics. Things could have gone terribly badly. But he wasn't about to go in that conversational direction with Poutine at this moment in time. Poutine was tops on the straightaway, but his cornering could be a little ungainly.

"Aw shit, they ain't gonna hurt each other …"

"Ross, I have to disagree. You should have seen it. They both wanted *blood*."

"That's kinda a com-pluh-munt, doncha think?"

"I'd very happily go uncomplimented …"

"Who is she?"

"I don't know. I don't even know if I *want* to know. Apparently, her name is Serena something or other. Bad news. She's been in trouble with the cops since she was a kid. I think she's a professional stalker or something. At any rate, she was naked and waiting for me. By herself. That takes balls! I have to conclude that she's dead serious about it. She must have seen the news coverage and gotten some crazy ideas …"

Just then a shapely woman drifted by, undulating in a very comely manner.

"Hi, Tony," she purred with a suggestive smile.

Vicar responded automatically, "Uh, hi there." But, after the words had come out, he took note of her posture and her eyes laser-targeting him. He felt exposed under a spotlight and turned his attention back to Poutine immediately, discomfort surging.

"Wow. She wantsa piece-o-you." Poutine was half admiring, half concerned.

"See? It's starting to happen everywhere I go."

"Wail …" Poutine yawned and stretched grandly. "I'd sayz ya better keep yer feet on th' ground. Stay close to Jacquie. She'll beat ya inta shape." He grinned.

A joke, yet it seemed right to Vicar. He pursed his lips and nodded in agreement.

"My worry is that she'll be frightened off. Weirdness is flying at us from all directions. I don't even know what to expect from hour to hour …"

Poutine just shrugged wordlessly and half smiled.

The waitress delivered two vodka sodas. "Courtesy of the gentleman in the corner." She pointed at the man with her chin. He smiled at Vicar, giving him a little wave with his fingers.

Vicar glanced at Poutine, whose face was scrunched up questioningly.

"You know that guy, Tony?"

Vicar waved and smiled back, laughing inwardly. Fibbing to Poutine would save a lot of awkward conversational heartache. "Yeah, yeah. We went to school together."

■ ■ ■

Serena was lying on a foam mattress on the floor of the microbus, thinking. Her minions were off doing her bidding. *Serena Vicar, Serena Kimi Vicar, Mrs. Serena K. Vicar, Madame Vicar, Mr. and Mrs. Anthony Vicar* ... She was beginning to feel more confident that Tony Vicar had the magic to carry her to the top of the mountain, above all the voices. Sometimes she talked back to them, but they said ugly things, and it made her want to hurt other people and herself. She turned on her side and caught a glimpse out the window of birds orbiting high above her; eagles, by the looks of them. She watched their dreamy circles, brought her knees up to her chin, and drifted off to sleep.

Vicar strolled over to the post office and checked the box for Liquor. A few bills, a small handful of flyers, and a handwritten envelope addressed in care of the store, but meant for him, marked "Private and Confidential." How odd. The return address was in Halifax, and the postmark confirmed it. Suddenly burning with curiosity, he started back toward the store, opening the envelope while he walked. A letter.

It was written in ballpoint pen in a light, shaky hand. Judging by the cursive the author was a woman, likely in her seventies. It was short.

> Dear Mr. Vicar, I have read about you in the papers and I wanted to ask you to help me. My husband is sick, and I am not strong enough to take care of him. Can you use your powers to do something?

Paper-clipped to the letter was a ten-dollar bill. Vicar stopped dead right in the middle of the parking lot, stunned. He began to cry.

Twenty-Four / Tight, White, and Strangely Right

There were eggs on the kitchen counter right next to a carburetor. The ledge over the sink was crowded with springs, levers, old screws, a screwdriver, and a stained easel-back calendar from 1976. That had been a good year.

Poutine sometimes soaked auto parts in the kitchen sink with acrid solvents, often while preparing food; not that he cooked *per se*. He did warm things up. Boil water. Fry something now and then.

The place was a dump. It was an old mobile home that he'd bought from a logger for five hundred dollars. He'd lived in it for decades. He'd put up a roll of snow fence around it in a lame attempt to fashion a front yard; flower beds — or a couple of strips of dirt, more like — lay awaiting something to be planted in them.

For some unknown reason there was a blue plastic kiddie pool and a couple of sun-damaged lawn chairs off to the side. Most would have described the place as a ruin, really, even though he owned ten acres of forest outright. Beside the portable was a rustic garage that held his beloved Chevelle and an array of tools and machines that would have left any backyard mechanic drooling. Nearby was the hulk of another Chevelle, stripped of parts and covered in an old canvas tarpaulin.

■ ■ ■

As she bumped slowly down the rutted path to Poutine's house, Jacquie O scanned the property. No goats in evidence. She wrinkled her nose and squinted. Surely, he didn't keep them in the mobile home. That smell had to come from somewhere, though.

Poutine came out from behind the Chevelle, which had its hood up. He leaned over and peered down inside, the crack of his ass writ large. Jacquie smiled.

A minute later, she followed Poutine up the aging wooden steps to his door and was immediately assaulted by the stale air inside. Cringing inwardly, she noticed that her eyes stung momentarily.

Whatever the name of this colour combo of beige and kitchen grease was, its patina emblazoned the interior of the glorified garage-cum-kennel. Gingerly perching on the lone stable kitchen chair, she began to speak.

"I'm worried about this weird woman, Ross. This Serena person. She is very dangerous." The hard, flat interior surfaces amplified her voice.

"Yup. I seen her hangin' around the shop with her gang a few days ago. She is ridin' buckshot over you guys."

Jacquie stared off to the right for a moment until she deciphered his most recent mondegreen. *Riding ROUGHSHOD. Right.*

On the wall was a *thing* … a crude attempt to construct a dreamcatcher, she presumed. It looked like it was made out of a coat hanger and some unravelled sock yarn. She was struck by the inexplicable concatenation of Ross Poutine and his homespun dreamcatcher. There was a clump of long, truly vile-looking hair hanging from it, too, and suddenly Jacquie didn't want to continue looking in that direction. The jarring incongruity of it all uncoupled her train of thought for an instant.

After a moment, she gathered her thoughts. "If she comes into the shop, call the cops right away, try to contact Con-Con. This woman could really make trouble for Tony."

"I figure it's *you* that's in trouble. Supposably she likes her a little Vicar. I think you might be in her road."

Poutine was right. *This guy.* Kind, generous, and surprisingly sensitive, but with the social graces of a bag of mud hitting the sidewalk from a great height. He was so rough around the edges that most people dismissed him out of hand.

Jacquie glanced over toward the end of the room and saw what appeared to be a small altar that held a few crystals and figurines, candles and incense. Despite their presence, her nose could sense no evidence of anything besides the usual pong.

She knew she'd felt drawn here to speak with Poutine for more reasons than his daily proximity to Vicar. There was wisdom bubbling under the surface. He just struggled to verbalize what he so accurately perceived. He was a man of simple, direct actions, not subtle, tactical words.

As for that horror show, Serena, she might try to manipulate Vicar, get him into bed. *But she probably wants to kill me. Like, actually murder me.* Jacquie wondered if the woman suffered from borderline personality disorder.

"I'll be careful, and I'll make sure the doors are always locked," she said.

"Weren't the doors locked at Tony's place?"

She looked at Poutine and sighed. He was right again. This was a dangerous situation.

"Oh, damn, Ross ... I don't know what to do." She put her hands to her head.

Poutine shrugged and looked around. "Well, you can stay here if you want ..."

Jacquie had to control her natural response to that. It was kind and generous of him to offer, but if she were honest about it, she would rather face mortal combat again than stay in a place this awful.

"Uhhh ... if I hide, then she's won, hasn't she?" She hoped this was enough to gloss over her unwillingness to stay there.

"Well if she comes at yuz, y'can defend yourself."

"I already defended myself. Look at the results." She still bore the discoloration of the blackened eyes.

"Aw shit. That ain't nothing. That's a Saturday night in Port Alberni."

"Betty, that must be the twentieth pair of used underwear I've sold today."

Elaine glanced over her readers at her fellow Goodwill volunteer.

Betty cackled and pointed out the glass storefront. "Look! They're wearing them over their pants, like Superman with a blown-out crotch!"

Peals of laughter erupted from the two middle-aged women.

The small herd of kids outside horsed around and laughed as they donned their new purchases. They were just following the latest trend. Wanting to emulate their local celebrity, the Liquor Vicar, they thought blown-out tighty-whities were the height of hipness, and good luck to boot.

▬ ▬ ▬

In the backseat, Jacquie was going over her to-do list aloud. "Celery, buns, Tylenol, post office … I think that's all of it. Too bad we can't stop and have a piece of lemon meringue pie." She cheerfully pointed at the old coffee shop, now closed.

Frankie Hall looked out the window of the Peugeot. "Did you know that Bill and I bought the Agincourt years ago?"

Vicar glanced at Jacquie as they passed the old hotel.

"We left Jack Dumont in charge, but we bought a majority stake in '72," Frankie continued. "And then we bought him out entirely just before Bill died. We had great plans for the place, but once he was gone, I lost interest."

"But I thought old Venables was the owner," Vicar said.

"No, Bill hired him to be the custodian and gave him a free place to live. He had a soft spot for the old coot. He was just a scallywag drifting around, doing odd jobs. I've owned it all these years. It's a shame that I never prettied it up, but it always seemed to pay for itself, even if it was ugly as the ass end of a horse." She snorted. "Men would drink beer standing over an open septic tank …"

Vicar chuckled ruefully. "Someone told me it might get demolished now that Venables is gone."

"I suppose that's possible. The land is prime and worth a fortune compared to the twenty-five thousand we paid for the whole thing back then. But I haven't decided, other than letting it close for the time being. I just don't want to keep it open without Venables. It's awfully rundown."

Vicar could hear the regret in her voice. It seemed that she had had plans for it all those years ago. But you could never know when your well-laid plans would be altered by an unforeseen turn.

They merged onto the parkway.

Frankie cleared her throat and said wistfully, "The only other place to get a cold beer now is way out at the Trapper five miles away. What kind of town doesn't have a beer parlour?"

She was asking rhetorically, but Vicar piped up. "It's not a town if it doesn't have a pub."

Farley could barely believe his eyes as he rubber-necked around Jacquie's house. It was so tidy! It smelled good, too. He had come over with Vicar for a little evening get-together. Vicar had brought some wine from the shop, and they were now gathered in Jacquie's cozy living room, sitting around the coffee table, which held a bowl of wax fruit. Vicar had made sure to point it out before Farley could take a bite. Next to Farley was an ornamental tree wrapped in tiny, cheery lights.

"Tony," Jacquie said, "this underwear thing is really, uhhh, weird. It's like we're living in a cartoon. Something really strange is happening."

Vicar had always felt life was a cartoon, but for him the last couple of years had been a gloomy graphic novel, better suited to angst-ridden outliers. "I know. Six months ago, I couldn't get arrested ..." He trailed off.

Now I'm a freaky superhero, my every word a pearl of wisdom. If I trip on the sidewalk it becomes a fad. Ugh.

They were all staring at the cover of a gossip magazine called *E-Obsession*, which featured a close-up photo of him and Jacquie leaving the grocery store — a baguette was sticking out of the bag and partially obscuring his face — followed by a small cadre of straggling onlookers wearing old underwear over their pants. The headline read, "It's Official! Liquor Vicar Shops with Jacquie O."

Vicar had no idea what that was supposed to signify, but he could see that they were already developing Jacquie into one of their front-page characters. He couldn't think of anything stupider than the utter drivel this tabloid published, although he had to admit that Jacquie was at least photogenic, and he was grateful for the heel of French bread covering part of his face. Never in a million years had he expected to see his photograph on a magazine cover, along with a splashy headline about Joan Collins's torrid love affairs, presented as if she had shagged Warren Beatty just last Saturday. He was becoming aware that some people actively sought out these rags and believed their contents. Such willing gullibility frightened him. The masses might be entranced by retro glamour, yet Vicar conjured a nightmarish collage: clicking, disembodied dentures with a mid-Atlantic accent simply *charmed* to meet Mr. Erectile Dysfunction in the form of a puddle with a knob. Cue the John Philip Sousa.

The denial of reality via believing in this patently fake baloney seemed awfully Orwellian, and yet it was a very successful arrangement. The tabloids counted on readers believing not that their headlines were completely true, but that where there was some smoke, there was probably a little fire. The understanding made everyone happy, except the people who were the topic of conversation. Vicar supposed that for some, this nonsense gave hope, or at least a needed distraction. But he couldn't imagine being so desperate, not even after some of his very dark days. He tried to sheer away from the topic.

Simultaneously, he was beginning to feel the effects of the cookie that Farley had given him as an offering of thanks. Farley had insisted that Vicar try one, so excited was he to be invited along to this get-together. Vicar had resisted at first. His history with this kind of stuff was iffy at best. But Farley didn't have much of a social life, and he'd hardly believed his luck at being asked to Jacquie's. Vicar saw Farley look at Jacquie and blush for what must have been the fourth time. So Vicar, reassured by Jacquie, who was on her home turf and in a happy mood, had ingested a tiny portion of Farley's "Space Biscuit."

Their entire conversation revolved around recent events. Wedding Elvis. The fight. The car accident. The funeral. The lottery. The stalkers. The heavy media coverage. Vicar wondered what might be next. Jacquie seemed less surprised about the attention than about the fact that Vicar couldn't see what propelled it. With her own eyes, she said, she had witnessed some stuff that was difficult to explain away.

Farley, on the other hand, acted as if Vicar had always had the key to all things, and he seldom questioned events. He unceremoniously flopped down on all fours, crawled to Jacquie's little stereo in the corner, and plugged his phone into it. Suddenly his arms and legs were thrashing around spastically as he sang about Tom Sawyer. Jacquie grimaced, no doubt wondering what other than drowning could prompt Farley to flail around like that. Vicar, on the other hand, paid Farley no mind. It was quite normal to have this kind of physical response when listening to Rush.

Vicar was unwilling to see himself as anything other than a run-of-the-mill guy and spent, he felt, a lot of his time being surprised that others couldn't apprehend what was obvious to him. He did sometimes wish he could be more easygoing, just go with the flow, be at peace with people's half-baked conceptions. But not, of course, if it meant swallowing the lurid claims of *E-Obsession* magazine.

Where the world saw magical powers in him, he saw nothing but an inexplicable change in his fortunes. Warily, he concluded that anything that meandered so randomly and mysteriously could just as easily turn back and flop. He'd suffer the slings and arrows of celebrity while he had it because next week, in a snap, he might revert to anonymous cipher, again left high and dry. At least right now, people were nice to him, and the band was doing fine. He thought about this for a second until his thoughts were interrupted by Farley singing at the top of his lungs, "*The river!*"

Vicar wandered into the kitchen, searching for a tin of mixed nuts, when the cookie really started to work its magic. He felt an odd surge in his body.

Pulling back the cupboard door had opened a portal to higher consciousness, or so it suddenly seemed. Staring at the snack shelf, he saw a deep-space view of a thousand or perhaps ten thousand galaxies, the image better and cleaner and sharper than any retouched deep-field shot from the Hubble Space Telescope.

Each galaxy was revolving like a top, its outer circumference rimmed by hot, glowing gases and dust. Star stuff. The kind of stuff that Carl Sagan had liked to talk about.

Vicar approached, soaring high above their plane and discovering each one to be whirling and rotating madly. He wondered, in his haze of pot cookie, how gravity held them together at that tremendous angular velocity. *This footage must be sped up for the sake of brevity*, he thought, hearing his own inner voice make the statement with just a little bit of reverb and echo. Flying closer now, he saw each galaxy as a constantly morphing Mandelbrot set, a digital representation of ever deeper resolution. Down he plunged into the heart of one digital galaxy, down, down.

Each galaxy was a universe of knowledge, a database, a billions-of-years-long collection of information, a spinning, starry hard drive. He found that each level of complexity revealed an older, deeper one, like a tower of champagne glasses receiving him as he poured and flowed. His fall was fast now, a rocketing downward trajectory through the very middle of the set into the centre of what he imagined was a black hole of pure mathematics.

He plunged headlong, spinning slowly the way a rifled bullet rotates, with one hand guided by a thread that seemed to run through all of this down into the midst of another galaxy. He fell like sand in an hourglass. Far beneath him, he could see yet another galaxy.

Beneath that, another, and then another deeper still, each a lower branch on some kind of tree.

He couldn't manage to grasp the mixed nuts, and he gazed at the oat and bran bars without recognition. Slowly he began to spin and rotate on the linoleum next to the sink, one hand up in the air like the spout of the little teapot. Jacquie stared at him quizzically from the couch.

Vicar's brain reasoned that at the heart of all this, there must be a starting point, or a finish line. Or something. Surely there was something. Everything he was aware of in this world had a beginning and an end. Why would it be different out there in the vastness of the universe? How could we differ from the universe that bore us? How could a son not be like his mother? An image of his mother zipped past his mind's eye: she was dressed in an old-fashioned bathing costume, and he was crawling toward her as she encouraged him with a singsong tone.

He plunged like a drunken Acapulco cliff diver, feeling his chest tighten, hoping his lungs and his brain would survive the fall.

As he moved downward, he saw the galaxies getting smaller, less massive, less significant, until they looked like simple thin strips, oversized, distorted pixels.

Suddenly he bounced, bottom-first, onto a soft carpet of balls. Pilates balls? Beach balls? He landed without injury and surveyed his surroundings: a huge, black, endless field of softly luminescent spheres. They spanned beyond his sight.

He spun around and saw the curvy thread that he had followed all the way down here hanging down a foot or two above the surface of balls. He grasped it and gently tugged downward, finding that it flexed easily. With both hands, he pulled until the thread touched the top of the bouncy ball beneath it. As it made contact, the ball shimmered and became a pole.

His perception changed immediately, as if the lights had just been turned on. Everything seemed different to him now.

He stared and cogitated for a moment. Why, they were not balls — they were zeroes! The descending thread had touched the zero and made it not into a pole, but into *the number one*! He was seeing the first piece of data; this was the very Olduvai of all information. He had just seen the original first impulse. Primeval digital. The om. The sound. The word. The voice. The big bang.

His mind flashed to the distant galaxies he'd seen at the beginning of the journey, and he knew at that moment that this very first non-zero, this first iota of data, the point of origin of all subsequent *ones*, was also completely analogous to the first binary fission of the first cell that gave rise to earthly life. Dumbstruck, he held on to the thread now attached to the *one*, leaning his weight on the strand that had guided him all the way down here. He gazed upward at it.

OMG … it was a double helix.

"Farley," he croaked. "Those are awesome cookies …"

Twenty-Six / Hospital

Frankie Hall hadn't made her usual wine order for a couple of weeks, so Vicar decided to check in on her. As he trundled the idling Chevelle down her driveway, he noticed that the garbage cans hadn't been brought in from the road. He parked and strolled back up the hill to fetch them. He pulled behind him the little cart the bins sat in, tucked it into the garage, and knocked on the door.

It took a while. Finally Frankie, normally cheerful and energetic, answered the door in a housecoat and slippers. She looked weak and was clearly not feeling very well.

"Oh, boy. You look like you might have the flu or something, Mrs. Hall."

"Good gravy. I don't know what I have, but I feel awful."

Her voice was pitched lower than usual. Her sparkle had always shone so brightly, but it was missing now.

She was ashen and drab. Something wasn't right. Vicar suddenly became worried.

"Can I come in out of the rain for a second?"

She coughed. "Surely, dear."

She stood aside to let him in. Vicar grabbed the phone out of his pocket and called Poutine.

"Hey, Ross, it's Tony."

"Roger, I gotcha five by five. Go, Tony!" Poutine replied, like a flying ace in a Hollywood blockbuster. Clearly, he was wearing his new headset.

"Look, man, I'm up here at Mrs. Hall's place, and she's not feeling well. I'm going to blow off my deliveries and take her up to the doctor."

"Uh-oh. 'Kay. That's affirmative, Liquor Vicar. Heh, heh." Poutine was delighted with his own comedy.

"If Jacquie can't cover for me, maybe Farley could do the last couple."

"Farley?" Poutine exclaimed, breaking character. "He's bolivious to everything around him."

Despite the worrisome situation, Vicar chortled. Farley was "bolivious" all right. If you stayed calm he was pretty good, but if you lost it around him, he'd start shaking like a dog in a thunderstorm. Vicar tried not to think about "Radar Love."

He got Frankie dressed and loaded her into the car. The Chevelle was so loud that she couldn't make heads or tails of his attempts at conversation. Already sick, she was badly aggravated by the sound of the car, which she called a "horrible crate." Vicar frowned uncomfortably.

Over the rumbling, he raised his voice and repeated,

"I said, we'll see if Doc Johnston will be able to help, and if not, I'll drive you down to the hospital."

The car bounced noisily past a couple of kids wearing underwear over their pants. Vicar looked at them in bewilderment.

"The hospital?" Frankie coughed again. "That's miles away. You'll do no such thing!"

Vicar just looked at her and gave her a lopsided grin. Folks as old as Frankie Hall were pioneers here on this island, where towns like Tyee Lagoon hadn't really existed until the 1940s. To a person of her generation, the thought of putting someone out over a cough was well beyond the pale. Then again, maybe she just preferred suffering in silence to sitting in this cacophonous car. It was probably just the flu, anyway.

Frankie's generation was a stoic one. If you'd told her about things like mental health leave or being traumatized by workplace harassment, she'd have reacted like a dog looking at a photograph of a cat. Blank stare. Going hungry and cold like they had during the bitter winter of '36 or losing your only child to some godforsaken battlefield — now that was trauma.

The doctor didn't take long to direct Frankie to the hospital. She briefly resisted, but ultimately retained that old-school deference to authority. You never went against the wishes of a physician, nor anyone in uniform.

"We can call the ambulance, but I know from experience that it will take about an hour, then it's another hour to the hospital." That was how it was out here in the country. The nurse was sympathetic, but she couldn't conjure miracles.

Vicar insisted that he'd get Frankie to the emergency room himself. She kept her fingers in her ears for the entire trip, except when she burst out in a rattling cough.

At the hospital, Vicar stayed with her until she was checked in and comfortable in her bed. By then, Jacquie had arrived. Frankie made a point of privately asking Jacquie to get her a few items from home, whispering confidentially and gesturing. Vicar stepped away discreetly, as if looking for something, while Jacquie listened attentively. Vicar's heart went out to this sweet old gal. What a shame she didn't have a daughter who could help.

"Should I call Pasquale?" he heard Jacquie ask gently.

"Oh heavens, he's in Italy for the rest of the winter. With his granddaughter."

"But I can send an email or call."

"Don't get the wrong impression. He is my gentleman friend, but that's about it." Frankie coughed again and covered her mouth with a fresh Kleenex.

Vicar returned to the bedside. "Do you have any family you want me to call?"

Without sentimentality, Frankie said, "Nope. I'm the last one hangin' around. Bill died of a heart attack in '80, and Billy was killed in 1951. He was a soldier."

Vicar was taken aback. He hadn't known she had a son named Billy.

"Korea?" he asked hesitantly.

"Mm-hmm," Frankie replied. "He was only a boy. Joined the Princess Pats."

She trailed off for a few moments as Vicar rearranged the items on her bedside table.

Then she whispered in afterthought, "He made it through Kapyong, but he died in some silly skirmish a few months later ..."

Serena had sent her minions out in the blue microbus to locate Jacquie O. The internet told Serena almost nothing about her, which displeased her greatly. Normally she could glean enough to wedge herself deeply into anyone's life. Not so in this case. A setback, but not a showstopper. She sorted through the case that contained her many wigs and brushed them out very carefully.

This Jacquie was a bartender, she knew that. She had asked around. The idiots around here were as co-operative as children, completely devoid of caution or suspicion. She could have made them tell their entire life stories. All she'd had to do was unbutton her top and question passing men; they'd volunteered tranches of in-formation based solely on a glimpse of her cleavage. She cornered one idiot, wearing an orange toque and Johnny Carson's discarded Bermuda shorts, who knew Jacquie. He was obviously a friend of the Vicar. But he'd been unable to clearly spit anything out, fixated as he was on her ample cleavage, as well the torn men's underwear she sported over her pants. Inwardly, she'd laughed as he hunched over, getting a boner. Pathetic!

Partway through their conversation, she'd realized that he was the bass player in Vicar's group. The one with the pompoms. Most of his information was worthless, just stuttering attempts to flirt. It would have helped had he been able to smoothly complete a sentence, but still, she knew how to tease out the nuggets. He couldn't remember exactly where Jacquie lived, because he'd been "wickedly fucked up" when he and Vicar were there. He had been doing some "bong hoots." All the same, he seemed strangely confident about her schedule. As far as where Serena might find "her old high school friend," he'd pointed toward a massive swath of forest on Royal Mountain. Searching all that might take days.

She checked her mobile phone again to see if Jeet had texted. Nothing yet, but she knew her target couldn't hide for long.

Serena was confident that she could have been a secret agent. But of course, she'd also have made a brilliant race car driver, or stunt person, or bounty hunter, or paratrooper, or so she thought.

It was amazing, how high you could set your sights when no one had ever countered your fantasies with reality. Serena was blithely unaware that though she was shrewd and cunning, she was also naive and ludicrous.

Beauty without smarts is a tragedy; beauty married to madness is a catastrophe.

— — —

"So what was all that about Frankie's son?" Jacquie asked. They were on their way to Frankie Hall's house.

"Billy Jr. She said he was a soldier in the Princess Pats. That's infantry, so he was a ground pounder. She said he made it through Kapyong. Korea. Crazy battle," he murmured, drifting off in thought.

Jacquie let him coast for a moment and then gently prompted him. "Crazy how?"

"A small number of Canucks held off, like, a million Chinese troops."

"A million?"

"Well, lots."

"So not a million, then?"

"Uh, no. It was like five thousand Chinese to seven hundred Canadians, or something. Nearly ten to one. But they held. Very few know about the battle. Crazy-brave old bastards." Vicar's head dipped as if he were bowing in respect for their memory.

"Wow," was all Jacquie could say.

They used the key Frankie had given them to enter the house. There was an unwashed mug in the sink, and Vicar spied all sorts of handrails and extra equipment in the bathroom as he glided past it.

The place was old now, probably sixty years, appropriately dark for a Tudor, but it had the musty smell that went with a seaside house. The axe-hewn oak and wrought-iron fixtures made it look like an ancient castle keep. The latches clanked, heavy and dungeon-like, as he walked through the doorways, worn flagstone under his feet. It looked a little like a fortress, yet it had a very happy feel about it. Vicar instinctively loved it. He imagined the cozy dinner parties they must have thrown as he passed a small, low access-door marked with a fading Scotch-taped sign that read, *Keep Out — Old Man's Private Stock — XXX*. The wine cellar, obviously. Old school. He grinned and climbed the steps to the main rooms.

The view was sensational, as it was situated high on a bluff looking down into the Lagoon; the sun rose to the left side of the window and set to the right. A thick forest of fir and cedar completely covered the side opposite his vantage point, revealing carved-out lots containing homes and garages. There were many now, but he guessed that when this place was first built it had been one of only a handful, and each home and family had had a private view of the sea and the heavens and the spectacular natural beauty of this barely known place. He was impressed; the house had been sited expertly. He stood for a moment and drank it in, even in the late winter drabness, as he leaned on the kind of fat oak post that Henry VIII might have once used for the *Mary Rose*.

To his left he saw a desiccated old upright piano. He lifted the fallboard and played a few notes — it was terribly in need of a tuning. On top of it were photographs from years gone by. Frankie, her hair dark and lofty, stood next to a man who was clearly her late husband. He towered over her as they posed against a giant colourful rhododendron. He was paunchy, wearing a loud shirt unbuttoned almost to the navel, like a seventies lounge singer.

There were several portraits in silver, oval granny frames, and one shot set in an ornate mounting that was both a frame and a vase. It contained a red carnation, quite fresh — it was probably changed frequently. The photograph framed within was of two soldiers standing on a city street, one in trousers, one kilted. The kilted one was Black Watch — Vicar could tell from his hackled Balmoral and the tartan. He had his arm over the shoulder of a soldier in a beret, with a cigarette and a pencil-thin moustache. A tall, skinny boy, he wore the cap badge of the PPCLI, Princess Patricia's Canadian Light Infantry. That must have been Billy Hall Jr.

Jacquie gathered toiletries for Frankie and then went quietly into the bedroom. Vicar could hear drawers opening and closing. He ambled to the kitchen and washed the lone mug. When he heard Jacquie make a little exclamation of alarm, he leaned into the room. She held a bunched-up pair of huge ladies' underpants that could have been used as a pup tent.

Looking pained, she said, "Someday I will have a pair just like these."

Vicar smiled. "I look forward to that."

For just a second, he thought he saw a blanket of warm colour throbbing around her.

Oxygen hissed quietly into Frankie Hall's nose while a monitor on a stand beeped every few minutes, creating an overlay of discomfort. Vicar sat in a chair beside her bed and gazed out the window at the drab evening sky, which was attempting to rain for what must have been the fortieth straight night.

He had learned how to read the monitor display and had realized Frankie's "blood sats" were low and getting lower. Her blood was simply not carrying enough oxygen. She was awake, but just barely, and her condition was worsening steadily.

Damned pneumonia, thought Vicar. What a crappy way to go. He'd had it himself as a young man and could still remember the wretched state he had fallen into, despite having been only twenty-two and otherwise in the fullest bloom of health. He recalled agony so intense that he'd required morphine. He gazed at Frankie with genuine sympathy.

With no motherly figure left in his life, Vicar had really taken a shine to Frankie, and being here with her now seemed the right thing to do. Plus, the quiet of the hospital gave him a place away from his troubles to gather his thoughts. And he had plenty of troubles.

He quickly reviewed his state of affairs. Jacquie was filed at the top of the Good column. She was revealing herself to be very special to him, although he wasn't the type to come right out and say it to her. He was never going to utter that nauseating "you complete me" shit, no matter how many rom-coms she dragged him to.

He did tidy up before she came over, didn't he? Well, sometimes. Surely that gave her a hint, right? But he was feeling increasingly comfortable being around her, more attached to the thought of her presence. He'd be happy to have her around for a long time — that was a first.

But there was a threat looming: Serena. What in hell's name did she want? Why had she set her cap for him? Not understanding was almost giving him hives. He couldn't help trying to analyze the situation exhaustively, from every imaginable angle, in search of the missing information. It seemed that Serena was determined to have him for her own, or at least to wreck what he was building with Jacquie O. And what exactly did she plan to do if she got her wish? These questions would not leave his mind. He was aware but not fully appreciative of the legend coalescing around him. All his years playing in rock bands had taught him little about the true source of hype and hysteria. He also failed to fully appreciate the pathology of Serena's deeply disturbed psyche. The only thing he was sure of was that, until Jacquie, he'd gone constantly unrewarded. He refused to examine things beyond that. *Keep it simple, stupid.*

He could hear the voice of the old Tony Vicar, pre-Jacquie, entertaining a reckless, self-destructive impulse to give Serena a go just for the sheer absurdist adventure and the tale he could tell about it later. Then he remembered the treacherous vibes she'd emanated, that sickly coloured, off-putting aura she'd exuded, those crazy-ass, deceitful eyes that had oozed a warning about a lifetime of misery to the fool who entered her web.

The new, changed Tony Vicar compared all of that to rock-solid Jacquie, who was beautiful and stable and uncomplicated. Her vibe was like curling up in your favourite chair. Warm, soft, and as familiar as your teeth are to your tongue. She was a Nelson Riddle arrangement, perfect from tip to tail, with a mind-blowing climax in the middle. She had certainly gotten under his skin. He knew that his bachelor days were over if he could pull it off. But he saw doubt in Jacquie's eyes at times; he wasn't sure she felt the same about him. This way could lie heartbreak.

Frankie began coughing again, an awful-sounding, rattling bark that made Vicar wince. The spasm lasted a full minute, and when it finally abated, Frankie's head lolled to the side in near collapse. The low moan that emanated from her made Vicar jolt upward.

Leaning over her, he put one hand on her forehead, looked directly into her half-lidded eyes, and wordlessly summoned something from within. He couldn't put a name to what he was doing, but he had done it before, just before Mom had slipped away, at the very end. The warmth of human contact, that was all. He just wanted to transmit vibes of comfort to this dear lady who was in so much wracking distress.

▬ ▬ ▬

She stands at a treeline, peering at a misty clearing. It is lushly green and seems to be undulating, as if she is viewing it through viscous liquid. She surveys it all for a moment, waiting for something. It comes. Unexpected, yet it seems to make complete sense. Frankie sees a large, dark moose running across the clearing from left to right, a blanket over its back, rich red in colour. The moose is majestic and powerful, moving with smooth grace. The colour of the blanket makes the running moose pop against the green background. The whole thing, Frankie muses, is Impressionistic, like a Van Gogh painting.

From the mist coalesces a figure, ghostly and glowing with energy. She realizes after a moment that it is her dearly departed son, Billy. His face morphs constantly; for an instant, the face becomes that of her father, dead so many decades, in his sweaty old Stetson. Now it is her long-dead husband, Bill Sr. He smiles, and she weakly tries to summon him back, but she can't muster the strength. Then her son reappears and reaches toward her. For an instant, she can smell him as a baby, the lovely fragrance of cut cedar and lanolin. She feels the warmth of his cheek on her lips. As he touches her face, he suddenly becomes Tony Vicar, hovering and surrounded by brilliant light. She doesn't know what it means, but she is not afraid. She is at peace. She and Vicar are suffused in a brilliant glow, until she can't see anything at all.

She falls into a comfortable sleep.

■ ■ ■

Tony Vicar finally took his hand from Frankie Hall's forehead. He put on his jacket and quietly went home.

The locals referred to it as the Diefenbunker, but it was no such thing. There was a bunker somewhere on the Island, but *this* structure was not underground, was not made of reinforced concrete, and it was fifty years older than any Cold War bomb shelter. In fact, it was the wrecked remnant of an old coal mine tipple, circa the First World War, now reduced to a trove of red brick and deteriorating lumber that slowly rearranged itself from man-made structure into random heap. A long-disused rail spur, overgrown with vegetation, curved past it. Rotting beams still jutted out from its interior.

Inside this ruin sat Serena and her gang of four. They crowded around a rusting sheet of metal balanced on top of a couple of old crates. On top of the makeshift table sat burning candles inside tuna tins and a copy of *E-Obsession* featuring a picture of Tony Vicar and Jacquie O.

One of the group, Dooley, was fiddling around with a flashlight. "I found out where she lives," he said.

Serena's eyes lit up fiercely. "Where? Show me on this map."

Jeet, her dutiful driver, looked around the dim interior of the demolished rectangle. This setting was awfully theatrical. Why not just rent a motel room close to a grocery store? Then he realized that he'd already asked that question, and his suggestion had been shot down in flames. Serena got him so muddled up sometimes.

This was where they'd keep Jacquie once they grabbed her. No one would see or hear anything. Jeet leaned over the crude map he'd gotten at the tourist information booth as Dooley poked a finger at what he thought was the location of Jacquie's house.

"What does it look like?"

"Little white house, short driveway right up to the front door," Dooley replied. "Not sure if there's a back way in, but the yard is private. There's a hedge around the whole thing. A couple of steps up to the front. Lots of windows, so we will have to be careful. There are a few other houses on that road, but they're quite far away."

With her thumb, Serena flicked the waistband of the powder-blue Stanfield Y-fronts she was wearing over her sweats.

"I wanna see it. Then we can decide on the final plan." Serena had several possible scenarios. "Tape?" she asked. She'd already decided that Jacquie would be bound and gagged.

"Check," one of them replied.

Jeet felt a little thrill and then hesitated, wondering why he was doing all this risky shit to help her bag some other guy.

As if she could feel his doubt, Serena turned toward him, flipping her long, curly locks — blond this time — and pouting her lips. She fidgeted with her unfashionable men's underwear provocatively, sliding her hand in and out of the waistband, and Jeet's doubt melted away like an ice cube in the desert sun.

▬ ▬ ▬

Frankie Hall woke gently. She felt slightly better, and someone had taken her off oxygen during the night. As she looked out at the first light of morning, she remembered her dream. She knew what she had to do.

Thirty / Irreversible Actions

Jeet switched off the microbus engine and rolled the last fifty feet to a stop near Jacquie's house.

There was a car in the driveway, and Serena felt confident Jacquie was home. She stood with her hand on the side of the vehicle, thinking and surveying the site.

"Andy, go through the bush and circle around to see if there's a back door."

Andy departed with a nod, and they waited. Five minutes later he was back.

"Small patio, sliding glass door. It's cracked open. She's inside. I saw her sitting at the table, eating."

They had several rolls of silver gaff tape. Serena gave one to the rear team and one to the front.

"Jeet, you stay here and make sure no one is coming down the road. Maybe turn the van around and get the door facing us when we come out. We'll enter from the rear, tape her up, and chuck her in."

"That's it?" Jeet asked, surprised the plan was that simple. He'd expected walkie-talkies and charts, maybe even toques and blackened faces.

"Yes, that's it. She's not expecting this. We'll rush her and get the hell out as fast as we can."

— — —

There was an awkward silence and then Farley finally spoke.

"She said she was Jacquie's friend from high school."

Vicar looked at him in disbelief. "And you bought that?"

Farley scrunched up his nose in discomfort. "Yeah. Sorry. I think I was high."

When aren't you? Vicar wondered angrily, but he knew it was Farley's go-to response, his get-out-of-jail-free card. He was far too old for this to be cute. Smoking up had been a carefree lark back in high school … then Farley had seemed to lose track of all the intervening years. For all his charm, the dude could be a bit slow on the uptake.

They stood in the kitchen of Vicar's wrecked home, the furniture still broken, the place still a mess, Serena's violent handiwork still starkly evident. Vicar looked at his feet and tried not to pity Farley. It was cruel and not the right response, anyway. Farley was decidedly sweet and gentle and childlike … but thick as a brick after smoking weed. Instead, Vicar tried to explain the situation to his foggy-minded friend as if he were teaching a child.

"Farley, ummm, you know that was the woman who broke into the house, right?" He gestured to the destruction all around them, elegantly sweeping his arms like a dystopian Carol Merrill.

Farley had been hanging his head in shame, but now he looked upward. "Oh man … I wasn't sure." In fact, he did remember that all he'd wanted was to prolong his time near those fantastic breasts.

■ ■ ■

Serena's gang — all wearing underpants over their clothes — poured through Jacquie's door and fell upon her like a pack of dogs. She began shrieking bloody murder and kicking her legs wildly, connecting her heel with the solar plexus of one of them. He fell back on the sideboard, blasting everything onto the floor. But before Jacquie knew it, she was completely bound, unable to move, and her mouth was covered with acrid-tasting tape. They hefted her unceremoniously and dumped her into the idling van, which hastily departed the moment its door slid shut. The entire abduction took less than sixty seconds.

Jacquie's violent protests were dealt with severely by Serena, who kicked and punched her when she tried to sit up. Jacquie quickly realized that staying still and mute was the smarter move. She was frightened, but her thoughts were still sharp. She determined to figure out exactly where they were going. She knew that if they headed into the bush, she was in great peril.

As they reached the four-way stop at the corner and made a fast right, a man looked out his kitchen window and saw an old microbus swaying wildly as it raced away.

He squeezed a teabag against his spoon and mumbled quietly, "What's your hurry, buddy?"

— — —

"Farley. We need to deal with this right now." Vicar's intuition told him that danger was afoot, and his heart was racing.

Meanwhile, Farley was sick at heart. The full picture was beginning to sink in. He felt a shot of adrenaline course through his body. He was frightened now, freaking out, and feeling an unfamiliar creep of anger.

Vicar may as well have been spitting out bullet points from a wanted poster. "You realize that this woman is highly dangerous. She's a stalker that levelled up —"

Farley liked to believe that like Bob Marley, he was a man of peace. But to be used as a tool to hurt Jacquie … *That is bush, mon. Not cool at all.* He felt quite ill. The rising nausea was nearly unbearable. His vision darkened. He slung his heavy backpack — weighted down with various marijuana paraphernalia, including a two-foot-long glass bong — over his shoulder and fell into deep thought. In a manner of speaking, the guitar cable plug slid into the socket, and he felt it click. In a flash, Farley Rea went from affable mascot to good man betrayed.

— — —

The road seemed to go on forever. By now Jacquie had realized that in her current state of anxiety, she would not be able to estimate how long it was. From watching the tops of the trees, she knew that she was headed inland, not toward the ocean. At one point they'd passed the industrial park; from her position on the floor she'd seen the top of the huge crane that was always parked there.

The brakes screeched, and someone swore loudly as another car's horn blew long, hard, and outraged. The microbus swerved heavily to the left and then went onto a gravel road. Jacquie's heart sank, but at least she knew where she wasn't.

"That asshole almost hit us!" Serena screamed.

I cut him off, thought Jeet, too intimidated to correct her out loud.

Then, suddenly, Jacquie figured out their destination. The Diefenbunker. All the kids called it that, though most knew it was an old mine structure. She was deeply anxious now. She thought about her mom. She wondered how many years it would take them to find her body way out here.

━━ ━━ ━━

In the hospital waiting room, the man felt around inside his tweed jacket pocket for the pen he knew he had put in there not an hour ago to ensure that Mrs. Hall could affix her signature. He had inherited Frankie Hall's file from his father, who had been her lawyer since before he was born.

Once she'd finished, he scanned the document one last time. "All right, Mrs. Hall. I think that's got it."

Frankie coughed painfully. "It's nice to finally have this out of the way."

— — —

Vicar got on the phone with Poutine immediately. Speaking as fast as an auctioneer, he tried to explain.

Poutine didn't completely understand, but he could hear the urgency in Vicar's voice. He caught Farley's name, and he knew it had to do with Jacquie. Jacquie was a filly worth protectin'. It was only thirty minutes to closing time, anyway, so he shut up shop early and revved his powerful Chevelle up the hill toward her house, which was only a few minutes away.

She wasn't answering her phone, and Vicar said he couldn't reach her by text, whatever that meant — more goddamn gadgets. No one had seen her today. And with that wacky witch wandering around, spoiling for a fight … Poutine took the opportunity to go as fast as possible; the Chevelle delivered both cheap wine and high horsepower. The speedometer read 80 mph by the second curve. He'd be there very shortly. *Goddamn that bolivious Farley.*

Poutine relaxed a little when he saw Jacquie's car in the driveway and the house lights on. He rumbled to a stop behind her car and jumped out. Bounding up the three concrete steps, he rapped firmly on the screen door three times. Nothing. He did it again. She might be in the can or dryin' her hair or somethin' …

He craned his neck over to the living room window and peeked in. He could see an overturned kitchen chair and a pile of broken dishes strewn about. Yelping in alarm, he attempted to enter. The door was locked. Without hesitation, he put his shoulder into it with everything he had and blasted through, ending up head-first on the loveseat against the far wall.

"Jacquie? Jacquie!" he croaked out as he tried to right himself on the soft couch.

She was nowhere to be found.

■ ■ ■

The driver's heart was beating out a tattoo. Red-faced, he turned to his wife.

"I'm going to report those guys!" he barked. He grabbed the phone, dialed 911, and described the reckless antics of the marauding blue microbus that had nearly taken them out.

His wife pursed her lips, smoothed out her tartan outfit, complete with tam, sash, and kilt, and shuddered as she realized how close they'd come to never meeting their first grandchild — hopefully a boy.

■ ■ ■

Poutine had immediately called Vicar from Jacquie's landline, which was upended on the floor. He described the scene: there had been a struggle, and Jacquie was gone. Her purse and keys were still in the house.

Vicar revved the Peugeot up to max, making it sound like an angry coffee grinder, and called 911 on the fly. He hoped Con-Con was on duty. He glanced at Farley in the passenger seat, peering straight ahead, hypnotized with anger.

"Move over, move, move!" Vicar shouted at the farm truck in front of them, puttering along in the early dusk. He blew his unimpressive European horn and passed on a double solid line, then tore up the curving hill in the fading light like a lunatic.

Two minutes ago, Vicar had hoped he might just be awfulizing. Now he knew for certain that there was terrible trouble afoot. He just hoped they could find Jacquie.

Thirty-One / The Bunker

Dispatch found Con-Con at home, making a nice birthday dinner for Nancy.

"I just got the strangest series of calls," the dispatcher said. "I think you need to know about this one, Con-Con. It's the Vicar and that strange stalker. They think she's kidnapped his lady friend."

"What?" Con-Con yelped, fumbling a wooden spoon. Nancy looked over with concern.

"Tony Vicar called it in and he asked if you were on duty."

"Good lord."

"They were up at the young lady's house. It's up on Royal Mountain, near the old mill. Cutter Road."

"I know it. On my way."

Con-Con turned to Nancy. "Emergency. Gotta go. Love you!"

She slipped into her Blundstones and flew out the door.

■ ■ ■

Vicar arrived at Jacquie's house to find Ross Poutine standing in front of it.

"No one inside." Poutine was in a state.

Vicar went in and surveyed the situation while Farley hovered outdoors, plainly upset.

Jacquie had certainly put up a fight. The kitchen was a battleground of overturned furniture and smashed dishes. He looked at the remnants of an antique commemorative plate for the wedding of Prince Charles and Princess Diana. It was split right down the middle. Vicar shuddered at the metaphor.

■ ■ ■

Con-Con ground to a halt and leaped out of her car, leaving her keys in the ignition and the door ajar. Vicar, Poutine, and Farley met her in front of the house.

"What's happened?"

"It looks as if someone took her forcibly. And I think we know who."

Con-Con entered the house and looked around the kitchen carefully. She was concerned, but very focused. "But to what end?" she asked finally.

Vicar shook his head. "I honestly don't know what Serena wants. I think she's fixated on me, or at least on all the stupid hoo-ha in the papers, maybe. I think she's totally out of her tree."

Who says "hoo-ha" anymore? Con-Con thought. And yet she found all the so-called hoo-ha awfully intriguing. The kidnapping, however, personally offended her. Jacquie was her friend, and Vicar had been her old babysitter way back. "Well, stalking is one thing, but kidnapping is entirely another level." Darkly, she hoped it was *only* a kidnapping.

Two police cruisers arrived, and she took the lead, explaining everything that the four of them knew. The Mounties were already well briefed on Serena and her hard-to-believe gang, having had a long laugh over the break-in and the home-destroying cat fight. Serena had been the talk of the detachment for some time.

The Mounties split up and began canvassing neighbours, asking if they had seen or heard a thing.

The old retiree on the corner said he hadn't heard anything.

"Nothing at all, sir? No strange people, no unfamiliar cars ..."

"Uhh, now that you mention it, I did see a blue Volkswagen van fly out of here like a bat out of hell a while ago."

Bingo.

The big corporal radioed in a report about the blue VW van and was answered moments later by dispatch.

"I just got a telephone report from someone on the highway saying a blue microbus nearly killed them when it cut them off turning up Harvey Road."

Con-Con and the two cops looked at one another.

"Harvey Road ... the Diefenbunker?"

"Got to be. Let's go!"

▬ ▬ ▬

By the time the hostage negotiation team rolled up in their convoy of vehicles, Vicar was barely concealing his desperation. It had been well over an hour since they'd found Serena and her crew, holed up and screaming bloody murder. The two first responding Mounties had cordoned off the area and made contact. But since then, absolutely nothing had happened. They'd simply listened to Serena's alarming and disconnected fantasy and kept her talking. They hosed down her fire with reasonable responses, if possible. It wasn't easy, because she was all over the map. And the more random her comments, the more tense Vicar became. What he wanted was for them to go in, guns blazing.

Con-Con was on point. She had a reassuring manner, but when the hostage negotiation team arrived, she reluctantly handed off her microphone to them. She sensed that a change might really throw Serena, but they were the experts.

It turned out she was right. In response to the new voice, Serena began shrieking, which scared the shit out of Vicar.

▬ ▬ ▬

Farley melted off into the dark, skirting around all the police vehicles and far past the loose cordon of observers.

Down on all fours, he crawled through salal and other underbrush a long way, until he found an opening that gave him a view of the interior of the tipple. He caught a glimpse now and then of Serena and her minions lit by flickering candlelight. Some of them were posted at little peepholes, striding around nervously and keeping their eyes peeled for encroaching cops.

Farley's view was limited, but he could clearly see the guy posted closest to him, at the opening. Not too tall or strong looking, the minion wandered around in circles, warily checking out the interior of the joint as much as he was looking outward. The police were all gathered to the front and unlikely to approach from this back-corner direction, which was protected by a cliff wall and heavy forest.

Farley waited and watched for about twenty minutes. He could hear Serena yelling through the slats and bricks to the negotiator, who used a scratchy bullhorn. Just as Farley was losing his small reserve of patience, someone came over and muttered to the lookout. Then, unexpectedly, the lookout minion put his leg through the uneven opening and gently probed for solid footing. He crept out, presumably to get a better view of the heat from the far side.

Farley tensed and silently unzipped his rucksack a few inches. The minion, in a crouch, crept from tree to tree. The tall second-growth firs were large enough to shield him from direct view in the cloaking dusk. He got so close that Farley stopped breathing and stood perfectly still. The minion was now only eight or ten feet away, crouched low ahead of Farley and looking in the other direction, toward the RCMP vehicles.

Farley hesitated. He was frightened, but angry. Then he thought about Jacquie, probably tied up in there and possibly in terrible danger. This was the moment when he could put right all his screw-ups.

He clenched his teeth, took two deep breaths, and lunged toward the unlucky lookout. *Not too hard*, he warned himself. That bong had cost him a hundred bucks. The wide base of the massive glass carafe made contact with the minion's cheek and dropped him to the ground with a muted thump and the crackle of crispy, waxen arbutus leaves.

━ ━ ━

Jeet had realized by now that Serena hadn't thought through her plan at all. The only weapon they had — besides the paring knife that had come blister-packed with the cheese they'd bought at the grocery store — was their wits. And when he looked around, it hit him that wits were in very short supply. He couldn't locate Marco and Dooley; they'd probably come to the same conclusion and snuck off, or maybe surrendered.

Jeet was beginning to see that there could be no triumphant endgame to this scenario. Serena would either give up and make this whole thing into yet another foolhardy adventure to add to her psychotic CV, leaving the rest of them holding the bag, or she would have to go through with killing Jacquie, her competition. Jeet failed to understand how Serena expected to be able to ride off into the sunset with the Vicar after taking that kind of dire action. And what was the all-powerful attraction, anyway? Vicar's band sucked, and he was old. What did the guy have that Jeet didn't? It seemed that Serena was just a fame whore after all. How pathetic of her, and how stupid of him. Jeet gritted his teeth and realized that he had been nothing but a dupe, a dupe who was surely about to go to jail for a long time.

He peeked out a knothole and saw a TV production truck and cameras and a gathering crowd, many of them wearing underwear over their pants. He looked down at the silly pair of skivvies he was wearing himself.

Frankie Hall could feel it now. She was slipping — her mind was letting go. Her will was leaving her. Her life force was quietly attenuating. Everything she'd wanted to do in these last days was now complete: signed, sealed, delivered. It had been a good run. A century was a long time for anyone.

A nurse drifted in to check on Frankie. She'd started refusing water yesterday, and her numbers continued to slip downward. She half opened her eyes.

"It won't be long now, dear," she murmured.

The nurse held her hand for a minute and then went quickly to the nursing station to find the contact number.

Thirty-Two / Downfall

Someone was coming to check on the lookout's progress. Farley saw the minion silhouetted against the candlelight, approaching cautiously, so he hid just to the side of the rough opening. The uneven bricks and wood provided some cover.

"Marco? Marco!" came a hoarse whisper.

Farley took a moment to decide what to do and then raised the huge bong over his head like an executioner's axe. From behind his cover, he grunted, and the minion cantilevered outward to locate the source of the sound in the deepening night. As soon as Farley saw the white of his skin against the forest's darkness, he brought the bong down in a vicious swoop, right onto the man's nose. Another one bit the dust. The minion fell limply over the lip of the wall, emanating a low moan, but not much more.

Farley vaulted over his body, bong in hand, and gingerly pressed his back up against the disintegrating wall that shielded him from view of the main chamber, where the shrinking gang was gathered.

■ ■ ■

Vicar was on tenterhooks back at the police cordon, feeding the hostage rescue team all the information he had. He was terrified that at any moment, Serena might snap and hurt Jacquie. His heart was pounding, but he stood very still, as if trying to convince a frightened dog not to attack, even though he was a hundred feet away from Serena, hidden behind a police van and cloaked by dusk. He looked around for Farley but couldn't find him. *Jaysus, he's probably off in the bush smoking a bomber.*

His phone rang. It was the hospital.

■ ■ ■

Poutine stood on the sidelines, leaning on his Chevelle, watching everything go down, and felt completely useless. There were a half-dozen cops — one guy with a shotgun, one with a sniper's rifle — blinding floodlights, and yellow perimeter tape. He wasn't sure what good the tape was going to do, but there it was. He followed its winding track around the Diefenbunker and spotted someone rustling around in the bush far beyond the rear of the structure. Everyone else's attention was directed on the other side. Poutine tensed … until he saw checkered Dacron slacks and instantly realized it was Farley. What kind of goofy stunt was he up to now?

Poutine surveyed the lay of the land and began making a wide, sly circle around the perimeter of the site. *I gotta git that bolivious twit outta there before he gets hisself shot.*

▬ ▬ ▬

Vicar clicked the phone off and bent over the hood of a police cruiser, resting his elbows and forearms on its warm surface. Noticing his body language, Con-Con approached, still in her civilian clothes.

"How are you holding up?"

"That was the hospital. Frankie Hall isn't doing very well. They want me to come in," Vicar said hollowly.

"Lord, things really pile on some days, don't they?"

"Mmm …" He closed his eyes and tried to control his surging anxiety.

One crisis at a time, he thought. *Let's just get Jacquie back safe and sound, and then I'll get up there as soon as I can.*

He looked around for Farley again. Still unable to locate him, he felt a twinge of anger that Farley could vanish at this crucial moment when he could have been providing support, however ham-handed. But then, Vicar dismissed his sour grapes, knowing full well there were far more important issues at hand.

He planted his feet in a little pool of semi-darkness, a private cove in a busy area, and began to mentally project outwards. He imagined he was connecting with Jacquie, with Frankie. Then he revolved around, within his mind's eye, to Serena. *Use your brain, Serena. Don't lash out. Just think it through and bring Jacquie to me. Just go easy and slowly walk out here. Give up peacefully.* He repeated this message several times.

Then he heard a voice. Imaginary, of course. A stress reaction. But it sounded like Frankie's cheerful croak. "All will come out right, my boy. All will come out right."

Vicar squinted and shook his head. *Man, the pressure is starting to make me a bit loopy.*

■ ■ ■

With the caution of a mouse, Farley peeked around the corner and saw Jacquie tied to a chair, her mouth covered in silver gaff tape. *Goddamn!* He almost yelped but stopped himself. He counted three people besides Jacquie. Two remaining dudes circled Jacquie ominously and hovered around Serena, who was turned out in a catsuit and a beaten-up pair of tighty-whities. Her hair was a different style and colour from what he remembered. That was one freaky chick.

Vicar was steaming. "Look, she says she'll swap Jacquie for me. It's *me* that she wants. You heard her. She said it fifty times. She wants me to be her husband or lover or some damn thing." He wanted to move this dreadful situation along more quickly. "If she wants me, that means she won't hurt me, right?"

But the RCMP hostage rescue team was firmly against a swap, hoping instead to wear the gang down from lack of sleep, food, and water. Con-Con did what she could to make Vicar understand the tactics, the methodology.

"The hell with all this fiddling around!" he said. "I am going in, with or without you."

"No, you aren't, Mr. Vicar."

"Well … then you'd better shoot me right now, 'cause here I go!"

Vicar charged through the undergrowth only an

arm's length ahead of one pursuing police officer, yelling, "I'm coming, Serena! Let her go and you can have me."

Convinced that there were firearms inside the hideout, the police fell back to safe cover, swearing furiously. Con-Con didn't even try to run after him. She knew the terrible risk, but she knew love, too. *Blind courage can be damned romantic*, she thought.

Inside the Diefenbunker, Serena's eyes flashed. She had won. She had won.

"This is far as I come until I know Jacquie is safe," Vicar called loudly from the entrance.

Jacquie felt the cheese knife at her neck — its pressure increased, her skin tightened. Her carotid was one tiny slice from being cut, and her epidermis was beginning to bleed slightly. Fear surged inside her.

Serena clearly wanted to have her cake and eat it, too. Hurt Jacquie, have Vicar for her own, and make an improvised getaway.

"Serena?" Vicar's voice was clear and confident. "I am not coming in there until you give *me* something. Let Jacquie go."

Time seemed to freeze, motionless. But finally, faced with this choice, Serena folded. "Fuck!" she exploded.

She started to cut the gaff tape with the cheese knife. It took at least five agonizing minutes to get most of it off. There was a further delay caused by her insistence on switching to yet another wig, in order to make the best impression on her Vicar.

But, eventually, Jacquie was walked to the doorway, her mouth still covered and her wrists still bound. Serena grasped her tightly from behind, still holding the knife to her throat.

Outside, the Mountie sniper trained his night-sight crosshairs on Serena and waited for the order.

Ignoring the peril around her, Serena purred, "Come over here, my sweet Vicar."

Holding out his hands in front of him, palms out, Vicar moved deliberately to within arm's reach of Jacquie. Her quaking and her bleeding neck spoke volumes. For a long moment, Vicar peered into her frightened eyes, attempting to reassure her wordlessly. He couldn't be that sure he was having any effect on Jacquie, though, and he was afraid to lose his concentration on Serena — she was an armed threat and literally inches away.

There was a pregnant pause, then Serena flung Jacquie away from her and grabbed Vicar by the collar, covering her body with his and poking the knife a little too hard into his lower jaw.

The sniper tensed but held his fire. No command came. There was simply no room for error, and apparently Serena was canny enough not to make herself a target.

Vicar yelped, and Serena pulled him backward into the building along with her.

Jacquie ran stumbling toward the nearest Mountie and fell into his arms. The huge moustachioed corporal bear-hugged her, spun his back to the threat, and moved her quickly to safety as easily as picking up a jar of honey.

She collapsed and began to weep as a paramedic extricated her from the rest of the duct tape. She couldn't believe Vicar had surrendered himself to Serena in order to save her. She was stunned, overwhelmed.

"Out of the frying pan, into the fire," the hostage negotiator muttered.

＝ ＝ ＝

Poutine was nowhere near as stealthy as Farley. He stumbled through the bush, tripping in the dark, making a racket that should have sent even the most aged and feeble forest creatures scattering. But there had been so much screaming and bullhorn crackling going on that he had managed to bumble up to the little portal — adorned with the drape of an unconscious bad guy — without being noticed.

Farley caught sight of Poutine when he was only a few feet away and frantically put his finger to his lips in a silent but desperate *shush*. Poutine, highly aggrieved by his stumbling journey and its attendant inconvenience, growled inwardly and moved aside so he could not be seen by anyone.

Farley watched as the baddies moved toward the far wall to scream back at the cops. He reached his hand through the hole and yanked Poutine inside the structure. The noise Poutine made was ungodly; hoarsely rasping curses like a longshoreman, his eyes burning with fury.

"Sonofabitch, Farley!" he rasped. "What the hell are you doing?"

Farley explained what he knew and that he had "improved the odds." Poutine immediately got the picture.

He looked curiously at Farley, who seemed to have transformed. Poutine wanted to do a double take to make sure this was the same guy he'd encountered two hours ago.

He was still mad at Farley for making him wade into all this crap, but since they were both here, he figured they could join forces and probably do in the last two goons. He was old, but he wasn't useless. And he was damned angry. His Levi's jacket was now torn to shit. *Goddamn.* He'd won it in a line-dancing competition in Williams Lake.

Thirty-Four / Cheese in Many Forms

"Don't be frightened, my Vicar. This is meant to be."

Serena's mad eyes seemed to be spinning and throbbing like fairground attractions as she gazed at him. Vicar knew in that moment that he'd have to step up himself and bring all of this to a close, without delay.

"With your power and my power combined, we can have anything." She wasn't exactly raving, but she was damned close.

Vicar glanced at the knife in her hand and swallowed once. He sat down in the taped-up chair, then launched into his plan.

"Yes, my love," he said. Hearing this, her eyes flashed like summer lightning. "I knew we were meant to be."

With that, she began to writhe, looking like a cat trying to cough up a furball. Her face flushed and her lips pouted. *Yeesh*, thought Vicar, *that's a bit much, isn't it?* Improvising now, he held out his open hands and extended cautiously toward her. He put one hand on her ample chest and the other on her abdomen.

"Can you feel our connection?" His question was as cornball as Darth Vader in drama class. He felt precisely the same as he had the day he'd fake-cried so he could skip out of school due to "a death in the family." He was nervous, but he forced himself to stay in control. If he maintained the upper hand, he could steer this, but if he lost his mojo, then she or one of her half-witted gang might kill him or someone else. He scanned the room for firearms and bolstered his courage by thinking about the sort of blockheads who took made-up stories from pulpy gossip magazines like *E-Obsession* as gospel. Maybe Serena would buy this …

She did. She began moaning orgasmically, her tighty-whities-clad hips thrusting. Vicar couldn't believe his eyes. For the first time in his life, he fully understood what it meant to be beside yourself. He felt as if he were watching the action from a distance, and he couldn't decide if it was hilarious, deadly, or otherworldly. He felt as if his body were being pulled long and tall, like he was watching a distressing optical illusion. His brain could not connect to the melodramatic hypersexuality displayed for his sake, or the surreal but deadly circumstances surrounding it.

"Sing to me, my Vicar," Serena whispered.

Vicar looked up at her, trying to hide his panic. "Sing? Now?"

"Sing now."

He couldn't tell if she was asking or ordering. Mentally, he was on Super Slider Sno-Skates and heading downhill fast. He skittered around in his head, desperately trying to remember a song to sing. Any song. He had to keep the ball rolling.

He squinted desperately, then flailed and grabbed at the only song that came to his panicked mind. Fixating on her long legs, he tremulously crooned, "… You are the wind between my knees." He whimpered the lyrics like some palsied Chris de Burgh at climax. Horrified with himself, he looked down at the floor, positive he'd really pulled a Farley. *Shit! I can't be serious even when it's life and death!* He began internally screaming at himself. For all that was holy, how had he dredged up *that* send-up? Nervously, he looked up, expecting a very bad outcome.

Instead, he had to quickly force his head and chin backward to avoid being whacked by Serena's spasming crotch. All the while, she brandished the fromage knife, slicing to and fro near Vicar's neck and face. Trapped in the sphere of her bizarre psychosexual dance, he gritted his teeth and hoped she wasn't headed southward with that damned knife blade. He swivelled his crotch as far away from her as he could.

Behind him, Jeet watched in disgusted silence. Such bullshit. *What a fake bitch.* Black, bitter jealousy began burning a hole in his brain.

Andy had taken notice of Dooley and Marco's absence and set out to locate them, though he knew it might be tough, because it was totally dark now. He moved deliberately so that the long, flickering shadows didn't trip him up. He peered out a knothole to one side but could see nothing.

Out the other side, he could see floodlights shining and police wig-wags blinking. But no one moved out there.

Jeet had the front covered. So, there was only the back corner left to check. Andy stumbled through the dark, brick-strewn passageway and spied the outdoors through the small portal there. There was some ambient light coming from the police cars, making his path easier to see. He moved down what must once have been a hallway between offices or machine rooms and picked up speed as he moved toward the window, just as the po-po blared their demands on the bullhorn again.

At that moment, Farley and Poutine both let go with their attack: a bong to the jaw simultaneous with the butt end of a two-by-four to the solar plexus. The RCMP blared something unintelligible, and Andy went down on the brick floor, not soon to get back up again.

Vicar heard the blaring bullhorn and its insistent tone. He knew it was time to move this drama to its conclusion.

"Now, my queen, we must leave this place." He feared he might be trowelling it on a bit thick, but then again, people seemed willing to believe anything these days. Serena's breath was heaving; he thought she might hyperventilate and fall over, and that would be for the best. The sad thing was buying his overwrought play-acting hook, line, and sinker. He looked at her with genuine pathos. She truly was mentally disturbed and needed help — long-term professional help. As he peered into her eyes, she seemed to change from a lethal siren into a needy little girl. He could feel her deflating before him. He would take her outside and gently deliver her into the arms of the waiting Mounties, who he hoped would be kind. It was such a shame that her life had led her to this. The tables had turned; it was he, now, in firm control.

Staying as casual as he had the nerve to be, he stood up and took the knife from Serena as if he simply wanted to unencumber her hand so that he could hold it. He set the knife down in plain view on the little makeshift table.

"Let's just go out there and make them take us somewhere nice."

"Now?"

"Yes, now. They can't refuse me, can they?"

"No. No. They'll do what you want. They'll do it." Serena was convincing herself that this was true. Everything would be all right. Her Vicar would fix it.

Vicar turned to Jeet, still brooding on the sidelines. "We are going to go outside. Do you want to follow us?"

Jeet turned away. "Yes," he said darkly.

Vicar and Serena turned around and faced the wall, beyond which lay the police and everyone else who awaited in suspense. "Okay, let's go out and do this," he said, smiling at her. She kissed his cheek and then the back of his hand.

The pair slowly moved to the entrance. Vicar was determined to exit first and signal that he was safe, that they should stand down from high alert. It occurred to him that he should call out loudly and warn everyone before poking his head out.

And then, Jeet called out from behind. "Serena?"

She turned to face Jeet, and in that instant, he plunged the cheese knife deep into the flesh of her shoulder, near the collarbone, as he howled a blood-curdling scream. Serena emitted an agonized wail and collapsed instantly, blood spewing everywhere. Vicar spun around, shocked, only to see Jeet yanking the blade out of Serena and turning on him. Jeet's arm came up, with the ludicrous but deadly fromage shank ready to do its dastardly work once more and be plunged into Vicar.

At that very second, from the shadows behind him emerged the wraithlike forms of Poutine and Farley, denim- and Dacron-clad, both swinging for the rafters. The sickening crunch that followed was heard as far away as the police cordon.

Jeet lay in a heap. Vicar stood a couple of feet away, white as a sheet and stammering. He could not credit what his eyes had just seen.

"Farley, you eedjut, you barked my knuckles." Poutine looked at his bleeding fingers and wiped them on his Levi's.

Farley was holding the stump of his prized bong, now broken in two, the bowl having blown clean off with this last swing. That bummed him out. He looked at Poutine's bleeding fingers and at the forlorn remains of the bong. "Oh man …"

▬ ▬ ▬

Frankie was all alone and slipping gently into the vasty deep. But she held on. She knew they'd come, and she'd stay until they did. That was her only concern now.

Thirty-Five/ Arithmetic of Aftermath

An ambulance had been ready and waiting at the Diefenbunker, so Serena survived the knife attack. Her carotid artery had been nicked, causing her to bleed profusely. It howled off at high speed as soon as they'd got her aboard. Her minions had to wait for more ambulances, but none of them was in any state to complain. To a man, they were unconscious, and the Diefenbunker was littered with recently "repurposed" teeth. Most of them suffered broken jaws, one of them a busted-up cheekbone, plus a small handful of badly distorted noses and cracked sternums. It was not pretty, and they were going to wake up in terrible pain. The Mounties were in disbelief that there hadn't been any fatalities in the melee; they even made a second sweep to be sure they hadn't missed anyone lying dead in the bush.

Jeet suffered the worst. The double smackdown delivered by Poutine and Farley had done such a number on him that he would certainly be eating through a straw for months. Vicar heard the paramedics bending over him gasp when he winced, showing that he was still alive. Jeet would forevermore bear the scars, physically and mentally, of his foolhardy adventure. There was no doubt that he was facing a long prison sentence, during which he could collect his thoughts and perhaps make a wiser plan for the future. *What a stupid waste*, Vicar thought.

He was sitting beside Jacquie O inside a police car, safe from onlookers, both staring straight ahead. He limply held her hand.

"She actually believed you could make the police go away and then take her off to some safe place?"

"Uhh, yeah." Vicar shook his head, feeling a sharp pang of sadness about the whole sordid affair. He had no degree in psychology, he had no expert knowledge, yet what was wrong with Serena seemed as plain as the nose on his face. He didn't need to hear the details about a wretched childhood or the betrayal of a father figure. He simply knew that the abuse you heaped on a child came back a thousand-fold. He imagined how much of a success Serena could have been, had her development not been cruelly disrupted. Dejected, Vicar turned his head and gazed out the window. He made out Becky and her mother in the crowd, standing behind the crime-scene-tape cordon and looking at him with big, silent eyes.

In a daze, Jacquie stared blankly at the scene, mesmerized by the pattern of blinking lights on the police cruisers, occasionally glancing at Vicar beside her. She was still shocked at how he'd surrendered himself to Serena's will, yet still come out master of the situation. She was deeply impressed.

The hostage negotiator, his square jaw set grimly, was trying to make sense of it, too. For all his training, he didn't understand at gut level what was wrong with Serena. Geared to think only pamphlet deep, his first instinct was that she lacked discipline or that her morality was flawed. Her long arrest record, he thought, was proof positive that she was just a bad seed.

But to Con-Con, it was like two plus two: good parents made good kids, who eventually made good grandkids. Not socially slick pretenders, flashy frenemies, but truly good and kind people, loving and selfless, folks who didn't mind getting their hands dirty even when there was no one around to ooh and ahh about it. Who you were reflected who your ancestors were, in a long string that stretched as far back as anyone could remember. Changing the route of that string took guts, brains, and a lifetime of effort. But it could be done. Con-Con had seen it happen. She hoped Serena could yank her string and bring everything back to zero.

Thirty-Six / Quiet Departure

Vicar and Jacquie hustled into the hospital, rushing as quickly as they could without making much noise. They were filthy, sweaty, and not at all emotionally prepared to see Frankie. Jacquie was a shaky mess, her hair gobbed with adhesive from the tape. Vicar's white shirt was spattered with blood that had exploded from Jeet's face. More than anything, they both needed a hot shower, a proper meal, and a good night's sleep.

Right now, Jeet was probably on a lower floor of this very hospital, being prepped for emergency surgery. Vicar felt an odd spasm of guilt, realizing that he didn't feel the slightest bit of sympathy for Jeet. That knife had been a half second from putting Vicar in his grave. Surely, there would be a heavy price to pay for that. Jeet could reflect upon his stupidity for a few months while his jaw was wired shut.

In Frankie's room, Vicar and Jacquie rushed to her and took her hands. Frankie opened her eyes a little.

Vicar could see the faintest glimmer of recognition.

"We're here, Frankie. Sorry it took so long," he said in a low, quiet tone.

He gently squeezed Frankie's hand. She didn't speak, but Vicar felt a weak, trembling squeeze in return. He glanced up at Jacquie, who had tears leaking out of her eyes. She had been through so much today, and now this. Vicar was afraid that she might collapse at any second, but of course, they'd had to come.

They stood awhile in thoughtful silence.

"Jacquie, I'm going to pop downstairs and get us a coffee, and maybe rustle up another chair, okay?"

She nodded with big, sad eyes. Vicar headed for the door.

"She's stopped breathing," Jacquie said suddenly.

Vicar whisked back to Frankie's bedside and felt her wrist for a pulse. It was fading, with only random spasms pattering. Her hand twitched a few times. Her chest was no longer rising and falling.

"I think she's gone." Vicar pressed his fingers against her neck and felt nothing. He looked at Jacquie and shook his head slowly.

They stood there feeling sober and sad, totally exhausted and slightly lost. Jacquie began to sob quietly, and Vicar wiped away tears, too. For just a moment he wished that he truly could summon spirits. But he refused to believe his own press. They would not come when he called them, of that he felt sure. All he and Jacquie could do was to hold Frankie's lifeless hands and absorb this latest shock. She had managed to hold on until they arrived, and then she'd let go, just like that.

After a few minutes, Vicar walked over to the nurse's station. "She's gone."

The nurse put a stethoscope around her neck and led the way back to the room without saying a word.

rankie Hall had planned her own cremation years before, but there was no next of kin to make any additional arrangements. Realizing this, Vicar called the funeral home. He and Jacquie would give Frankie a proper memorial service when they could do so without the careless disruption of TV production trucks and uninvited visitors in used underwear. They would scatter her ashes later, when the time seemed right.

Vicar was glad that he had been there for Frankie's last moments, but this knowledge did little to fill the hollow, lonely feeling that sat in his gut.

The press's relentless hounding had started to abate slightly, thank God. Jacquie and Vicar still couldn't go home, though — there were camera crews and reporters staked out everywhere. After a quick huddle, they both agreed to hide out at Frankie's place until interest waned enough that they could move freely around town. For now, the news crews mostly wandered around buying fancy coffees and frequenting Liquor to see Ross Poutine, who had agreed to let Vicar take a couple weeks' leave. They fairly pounded him for details, but Poutine was cagey.

"You wanna talk to me, you gotta buy somethin'." Poutine had seen his advantage immediately.

"Okay, I'll take a six of that lager," said the field reporter, pointing at a display.

"A six? So, you want me to grunt?"

The reporter knew he was beaten, and Poutine pushed it to the extreme, making everyone on the crew buy a dozen craft beer each. There were four of them if you included the tech. Word got around that this was the way to his heart, and then all the media were trying to outbid each other for interviews. Poutine was having a helluva good day.

▬ ▬ ▬

Vicar and Jacquie watched with amusement Poutine's interview on the TV at Frankie's.

"Oh, sure! I know 'em well. You know, Tony Vicar works for me. I sorta discovered him. Learned him all about the liquor biz-nuss. Jacquie? Oh, she's good people. Cutie. Smart, too. She knows dem computers, dere."

Poutine slapped his hand on the monitor at the cashier's counter with a cocky confidence that made Jacquie and Vicar cackle.

The reporter, an intelligent, elegant, and drop-dead gorgeous woman with an artificially low alto cadence, asked, "But what can you tell us about Tony Vicar's rumoured powers? That he seems to have some unusual metaphysical gift or talent."

Poutine looked at her like an old, sad-eyed hound.

"Uhh, ya mean all that hocus-pocus?"

The reporter smiled encouragingly. "Yes."

"Mmm. Well, I know it's all true. Spooky shit. Bringin' 'em back to life, makin' that dingbat Amazon calm down. Myself, I use a two-by-four" — Poutine swaggered, bringing up his part in the big hostage situation — "but he's got mysterious ways, that Vicar."

Vicar gasped. "Oh no, oh no! This is going to go international. Now everyone is gonna believe that nonsense."

Jacquie just looked at him for a long time.

Thirty-Eight / The Axis of Tweed

He stood up and put on his jacket, so that when he met her, he wouldn't be in just his sport shirt. The jacket didn't so much make him look more impressive than it did improve his confidence, as if he were a soldier in proper dress uniform. Besides, half his clientele had been handed down from his father, and they had certain notions about how a lawyer should look and act. It was a pain in the ass some days, but people definitely reacted positively to tweed. *Don't mess with a proven winner.* He smiled to himself.

Out in the waiting room, Jacquie wondered what all of this was about. She had been through so much in the last few weeks that she'd begun to stumble through her days, slightly disconnected from the constant activity. She could go out to town now, although she'd be instantly recognized by nearly everyone. Most had moved on from the underwear fad, though it hadn't fully run its course yet. Today she'd seen one guy walk out of the hardware store still sporting them.

At least the photographers appeared to have folded up their tents and left town. However, any new activity on Vicar's part would be reason enough to scramble the whole wretched lot of them again. And there was one crew still skulking around, trying to make a documentary about him for some paranormal channel.

"Miss O'Neil? C'mon in." The lawyer introduced himself and sat her down in front of his desk. "You are no doubt wondering why I called you in, and why I've kept this so mysterious."

"Yes, I am very curious, to say the least." Jacquie opened her eyes slightly wider and leaned in toward him, prompting him to quit stalling and cut to the reveal.

"It's confidential, of course, and seeing that you were under the microscope of the media, I had no desire to make them aware of this unrelated matter. I have here a last will and testament in the name of Mrs. Francis Edna Hall of Tyee Lagoon, who has named you the executor of her estate."

Jacquie sat up, not at all poised — her jaw was agape, and a slight grunt emanated from it. "Frankie? Executor?"

"Yes, Mrs. Hall called me to her bedside only a few days before she passed, and finally updated her will. She hadn't done so since her husband died. When I first took over my father's practice, I reminded her that her will was decades old. But she'd delayed it all this time because she had no living family to manage her estate after her death, save a few distant cousins. She explained to me that she felt you would be best suited to executing her will and disbursing her earthly belongings."

Starting to catch up now, Jacquie realized that at the end, she had been the person Frankie trusted most to follow through. Her heart swelled with affection for that wonderful woman who'd taken her in so quickly, and so close.

"Of course, I'll do that final job for her. It would be my honour."

"Thank you. I'll show you the will, then."

The lawyer read his copy aloud while Jacquie skimmed along. She slumped in shock as she learned that Vicar had been willed full ownership of the Agincourt Hotel, and that she herself had inherited the house on the hill overlooking Tyee Lagoon — 411 Sloop Road, Frankie's private home and residence for nearly sixty years. Some other items were to be distributed between a small handful of people, including her and Vicar.

Trying to stay focused, Jacquie inspected the long, detailed list again.

"I wonder why she's giving me the house and Tony the hotel?"

The lawyer laughed. "She said, 'God himself couldn't keep a house as well as a woman.' She also said *he* had talent, but only you could give him a home."

Tears fell down Jacquie's cheeks as she laughed a little. Frankie's tremendous generosity was hard to take in, and it had been accompanied by her characteristic wryness. To her thinking, God was apparently a man; ergo, he was a slob. What an old-fashioned but touching way to express her feminism.

Jacquie understood in that instant that Frankie had not only seen the future, she had also been intent on creating it.

"What? What?" Vicar knew something was up, but he couldn't read whether it was good or bad. "What's happened?"

"Well, uhhh …" Jacquie paused to find the right words. Her eyes were puffy from crying.

"Jacquie! What is it?"

"Mmm … Frankie made me executor of her estate, and she's left you the Agincourt Hotel." She waited for his response.

"She *gave* me the hotel?" Vicar asked. Jacquie just nodded her head. "Gave it to me, lock, stock, and barrel?"

"Yes. And she gave me this house." She glanced around the kitchen — which was now hers. She was in somewhat of a daze at the thought.

Vicar stood silent a few beats, looking around the house as well. It was a huge, homey, rambling manse. As a little boy, he'd always wanted to live in a castle, and this felt awfully close. He'd fallen in love with it from the first time he set foot inside. He pawed through his brain, struggling to find something useful to say.

"It's, ahhh … pretty old. Couldn't she at least have given you a *new* house?"

Jacquie fell against him and began sobbing.

Vicar was so thoroughly taken aback by the news of his surprise inheritance that he had to vacate the house and clear his muddled thoughts. He wandered down Sloop Road and stopped off at Archie Muir's place. Archie was an old widower who lived with his Dalmatian. Vicar had delivered vino to him many times. On occasion, the dog's incessant baying had made it almost impossible to transact the delivery.

"Hey, Arch, I'm going for a hike. Do you mind if I take Dickie with me for a workout?"

"Aye," Archie replied in his Highland burr. "He needs a r-r-run, and my hip's total shite."

Vicar let Spotted Dick off his lead and wandered off at a good clip into the forest trails, heading downward to the ocean. The Dalmatian was far too delighted with his adventure to stay on a straight course.

"Dick, come! Dick! Come!" Vicar yelled, just as two strolling ladies approached. They gave him a wide, cautious berth and made sure to watch him over their shoulders as he continued down the path. Vicar shook his head ruefully, thinking of Archie's Glaswegian sense of humour. He'd probably named the dog for just such a scenario.

The cool trees shadowed the rooted path, requiring Vicar to keep his eyes on his footing until he came to a clearing that overlooked a magnificent view. He stood awestruck at the sheer beauty of the precipitous hillside plunging down into the undulating Pacific. He had travelled and seen some of the world, but never really lived anywhere else, and yet still he was overwhelmed by the unspoiled beauty of the view before his eyes. He traced the coastline to the distant point that bordered the Lagoon and could see the roofline of what was now Jacquie's house. Glancing seaward, he spied the pastel hummocks that were some of the Gulf Islands, little communities of their own that looked to him like mere purplish humps. With the mountains of the Sunshine Coast as a backdrop, a lone tugboat pulled a log boom in the strait, leaving an ever-widening wake that rippled the water for what looked like a couple of miles. Stock still, Vicar simply breathed and listened. The powdery, earthen aroma of moss and fallen fir needles mixed with the gentle scent of kelp. The buzz of insects, the taunting caw of a crow somewhere nearby, the whisper of the boughs swaying in the gentle sea breeze, the lapping whoosh of the ocean down beneath him — all combined to play a quiet symphony. Only a few minutes of this would last him a long time.

His thoughts drifted to his improved circumstances. He was a multimillionaire, just like that, the owner of a hotel and the block of property it sat on. He had never had two nickels to rub together before; now he had a life's fortune laid at his feet. This was an entirely new level, a plateau he'd never found a route to reaching on his own. He felt like an eleven-year-old standing at the foot of a rocket to the moon. Someone had just given him a first-class ticket for it.

Vicar allowed the luxuriant feeling to wash over him for a few minutes, then pushed it aside when doubts rose up from the depths of his psyche. *You're being far too self-critical*, he admonished himself. *Just enjoy it for a few minutes!* But it seemed fair to wonder whether he had the ability to maintain all this, now that it had plopped into his lap, considering he didn't have it within himself to acquire it all under his own steam.

Vicar gritted his teeth, realizing that he was already whining like a rich person. *My lord, they live in total terror, don't they? Well, fuck that.* He was finally in a position where he could be the anchor point of an extended family, a head honcho. Not some kibitzer hovering around on the periphery. Frankie had once hinted at his path. "What kind of a town doesn't have a beer parlour?" she had asked him.

He replied out loud, telling the trees the same thing he had told her: "It's not a town without a pub."

He looked around for Dick the Dalmatian and headed back to the house where Jacquie O and his future lay.

Forty / Famine and Feast

Vicar was conjuring a hundred different possibilities for pub design. A quick cast around the internet had led to hours of research and countless requests to "Look at this website!"

Jacquie was doubtful, as Vicar was scattershot. Too artistic for her tastes, and bizarre at times. She knew he was brimming with enthusiasm and energy, but she could seldom see how he could make any of his many, many dreams practical, profitable, or, hell, even doable. The building could bear only so much change. The laws of physics were immutable. But still, she looked, keeping the peace while simultaneously trying to track his giant spasms of creativity.

This time, however, she saw something that seemed to be on point, at least.

"These are really beautiful," she said, admiring before-and-after photographs of pub renovations. They had the added appeal of being realistic, a quality Vicar could sometimes omit. She tried to recall the beer parlour's size and shape, to the best of her recollection, and compared them to the shots she was looking at. "You know, if we decide to renovate, it's going to cost a fortune. And one fortune might be enough to refurbish the beer parlour, but what about the coffee shop? It was already a wreck twenty-five years ago. The linoleum is worn black in places — it has been since I was a teenager. The ladies' room is vile. We would probably need a completely new kitchen, and of course everything in the dining area needs to be ripped out and replaced. There are Waring blenders in there that make me want to wear saddle shoes ..."

Vicar's vivid imagining ceased as he began to glumly consider what Jacquie had said. It seemed clear that she was leaning toward selling the whole property. He hated practicalities that doused his enthusiasm. Couldn't a man dream a little?

"If the coffee shop is too much for us, how could we manage a whole hotel? That would probably cost a gazillion bucks!"

"But we might be able to make money on a hotel, don't you think?" The disappointment she'd seen on his face made her want to try to be positive.

"Make money on a hotel? Have you even vaguely done the math on that?"

Vicar rolled his eyes as if in possession of secret insider knowledge. He had none, but you didn't have to be a rocket surgeon to see that from November to May, you could practically use the streets of Tyee Lagoon for bowling. No customers meant no business — that was all you needed to know about that.

Jacquie had to admit that they'd need to take out a huge loan against the property to make the hotel feasible. Could they do it on their own? Her thinking stopped short of involving investors. She veered away from any scenario dependent on shadowy shareholders, knowing instinctively that "backers" were people who either backed out or stabbed you in the back. Perhaps their idea was unworkable, and they should just sell the property and the old building to some huge hotel chain.

For days they left things there, high-centred between fear and fantasy, ironically feeling down in the dumps about the feast being served at their table.

Forty-One / Named After a Battlefield

Vicar wandered around the interior of the Agincourt Hotel and let his thoughts roam. It was a colossal hulk, really. Old and decrepit, but it had been in service until just last year. He marvelled at how rundown a building could be, yet still remain in business. The elevator had ceased working a decade ago, a dormant brass antique that whispered of grander days. The stairs creaked and were badly worn. Vicar was worried he'd crash through the steps leading up to the third floor and possibly end up injured and stranded in a locked, empty building. He really shouldn't have been alone in a place so rickety. He climbed the stairs cautiously, his feet splayed out to the sides of each step for maximum support.

The entire third level had been shut down years ago, and the floor creaked loudly underneath him now. At one point the sounds produced by the floor and one of the doors combined into something terrifyingly close to human speech, a disembodied "Who are you?" Vicar whirled around and thought he glimpsed something black and ominous, but finally concluded that his imagination was getting the better of him in the dim light. People had been telling ghost stories about this place since he was a kid. The legend was stuck in his brain, that was all.

At any rate, the third floor was dire, uninhabitable, and tinged with a vaguely malevolent feeling. It made him think of Spahn Ranch, absent only Charles Manson and his gonorrhea-ridden harem of murderesses.

He carefully descended and found the second level, with its ragged remnants of hall runners tangling in his shoes and its chipped-up doors with missing stick-on room numbers. It was unserviceable, and it creeped him out.

The ground floor, well … It still contained the old coffee shop and the beer parlour on the other side, but the state of both was sad indeed. In the beer parlour, the smell of beer and cigarettes stung his nostrils. The odour was universal, and universally depressing. Surely there was a way to avoid having a pub smell like it was flooded with beer dregs. Why was it that you never noticed that honk when you went in, thirsty for a pint?

He strolled up to the bar, the ugly contraption that they had unwisely installed thirty years before. It was piled high with old-style beer glasses stacked in plastic racks, ready to be filled with beer immediately, if you could overlook the thick layer of dust. The taps themselves had been secured as if for the night, but in fact, one night had turned into a year. The stylish handles had been unscrewed and stowed away safely. Pawing through the drawer, he saw only one or two types that he liked.

He looked at the ceiling: needed a redo. The floor: same. Walls: egad. The lighting: ugh. The wagon-wheel chandeliers would *not* cut it. The old, round tables were still covered in elastic-fitted terry tablecloths. Horrible. The door was reminiscent of a prison entrance; it was surrounded by a steel insert that had obviously been made by a drunk welder, or perhaps a blindfolded one. He could easily imagine the whole grotesque thing having once been covered in boiling oil and assaulted by the catapults of the Teutonic Knights. It must have weighed four hundred pounds and probably could withstand a direct hit from a tank. The rest of the building might collapse, but the door would hold firm.

In the corner was a vending machine still containing some snacks and chocolate bars. By now they would be hazardous to the health of even marauding raccoons — evidence of which was mercifully absent.

Vicar felt serious doubts arising about the resurrection of this old'joint. It just seemed a bridge too far. Maybe they should just sell the property, cash out. But to be replaced with what? Fast food? A big box store? Overpriced condos for elderly people who would keep watch through binoculars for encroachers upon their private parking, even though they didn't have cars anymore? After all, the kids had *promised* to come by for a visit.

As he crept down to the basement, his heart sank even lower. The storage area, home of all the kegs, was a dank, terrifying warren of potential slips, falls, and concussions, and Vicar was positive that it was a haven for rats. His little flashlight barely carved through the gloom, but, revolted, he could hear an unwholesome skittering.

His phone rang. Jacquie and Poutine were at the door, wanting to see the place. Vicar climbed back up the steps from the cellar and wandered to the back entrance to let them in.

As they toured the building, Jacquie became increasingly alarmed at the state of disrepair.

"Are you sure this hasn't been condemned?"

Vicar knew she was joking, but still hesitated. "Uhh … I don't *think* so. Wouldn't there be a sign posted somewhere?"

"Yes, the difference between a grand hotel and a condemned building is a sign posted in a central location," Jacquie said sarcastically.

They both laughed. Jacquie picked her way through the coffee shop as if walking through a field of cow patties, wary of the detritus littering her path. Near the doorway, she jumped back with a little gasp.

"Aaah! Is that a crab?"

She was looking up at a cobweb of gigantic dimensions, in the centre of which sat an arachnid of epic size. It looked as if it could kidnap a calf with ease.

Vicar had never been afraid of bugs, but he was nonetheless impressed with this one and gave her a wide berth. What in heaven's name had she been dining on to get that large? The spider just sat there motionless, like an eerie surveillance camera, staring at her environment, primed to attack at the first indication of incoming snacks. Sitting in her web, she looked like a giant wall hanging that you might find at the home of your slightly barmy aunt. When the time was right, Vicar would move Madame Spider to new digs, but for now, he decided she would be an unofficial mascot.

They peeked through an opening and saw that the coffee shop kitchen had made food for the beer parlour, too. Staff would have simply passed plates in one direction or the other, depending on where the order had come from. It must have made for a busy kitchen.

Some days had been nuts at the Agincourt — like payday. All the town's residents knew to stay clear because you'd never get a seat unless you were a big, loud, thirsty logger, and by closing time you'd probably need an ice pack for your injuries. Those days were gone, but the memories, and perhaps a few of the marks, lived on.

Poutine had blown several of his paycheques here and had some fond recollections. He may not have made the smartest use of his time back then, but those were the only salad days he'd ever have, so he filed them under "good memories." But even he had to admit that they'd spent most of their days well past the line of sobriety and good behaviour. Decades later, he knew the difference between a joke and sheer cruelty, but back then he probably hadn't been too clear. None of them had been. His first broken leg had been the result of a stupid prank by his buddies who were three sheets to the wind, guffawing smugly and lashing about drunkenly with chainsaws. He broke his leg running from them, but it could have been worse — much worse.

Jacquie, Vicar, and Poutine pushed through the swinging kitchen doors and bumped around in the half dark. The kitchen was well used, indeed, and would need a major makeover before it could operate again. That was if the structure itself could pass inspection. They peered into vats and stoves and ovens and grimaced at the collected filth of the commercial kitchen. Jacquie couldn't believe that she'd sometimes come in here thinking it'd be better than cooking for herself.

Another pair of swinging doors took them into the beer parlour — they entered right beside the ghastly metal-and-glass bar that Vicar so despised. Jacquie looked at the jumble on the floor, the overturned chairs, the cardboard boxes partially filled with junk, and felt her stomach sink. The inside was worse than the outside, which looked as drab and unappealing as a dinner accidentally dropped onto the floor. The building had been painted a shade of pink that had no doubt been charming and fashionable at one time, but it had faded unevenly over the years to give the place an air of abandonment. It was reminiscent of a gone-to-seed drive-in theatre somewhere in the lonely desert. Someone had repainted up to eye level in a tedious beige, and even that coating had grown mouldy and faded, leaving the entire outer structure looking fire singed and bomb damaged.

Jacquie wrinkled her nose. No matter how you sliced it, this would be a big job. Even if Vicar wanted to knock it all down and start again, the demolition would be a huge endeavour and not something that either of them had any experience with. She herself certainly didn't know where to start. She gave Vicar a quick glance and then looked away again. This was starting to feel like a great big fat white elephant that they'd have to fish out of a money pit.

Meanwhile, Poutine was stuffing quarters into the antique vending machine and repeatedly pulling the plunger, having found the cord and plugged it into the wall. He rapaciously gobbled the well-past-expiry-date treats, one after the other. Jacquie covered her mouth and winced as he fairly inhaled a Twinkie that was at minimum one year old, although who honestly knew how long it had sat in that old machine? It might have been languishing in there since the Great Depression, for God's sake.

Little bits of cake gobbed out of Poutine's mouth as he blurted out, "I *love* this place!"

Forty-Two / Caduceus Oil

Vicar was deeply lost in thought on a very slow day. The weather was poor, and no one was venturing outside, or so it seemed. As he stocked the shelf with gin, he was surprised by a customer who seemed to suddenly appear. Vicar hadn't heard him come in.

"Word is you're the new owner of the old Agincourt, Mr. Vicar."

It was common knowledge now. Vicar glanced up from the box he was unloading. "Yes, yes, I am. I'm still wondering what to do with it. It's awfully rundown."

"Well, you could refurbish it, couldn't you?"

"Oh, I suppose so, if I go into debt up to my eyeballs and then some. I just can't see that being sensible in a place that's so seasonal."

The customer looked vaguely familiar. He seemed wise to the topic and made some valuable observations, which Vicar found a refreshing change to the unhelpful responses of blithe, untethered enthusiasm he had gotten from most everyone else except Jacquie — and she was perhaps a little too realistic about the risks.

"But you see, the main attraction would just be the pub, and there's only so much pull you can exert way out here in the country …"

Vicar trailed off. Everyone here knew the vicissitudes of rural, seasonal life. It was a constant worry.

"I think you might be overlooking the obvious, Tony. May I call you Tony? I'm Gary."

They shook hands. Vicar looked down at Gary's incongruous snakeskin boots. How unusual.

"The way I see it, *you* are the big draw, not a cold pint of beer. You are the Liquor Vicar to a lot of people. They know about your amazing skills."

"Man, oh man … That's all hoo-ha. I'm just a guy."

"I wouldn't say that. I know the stories. They're building a legend around you. And legends can be powerful," Gary said. "You're a music fan, aren't you? Two hundred years ago, newspapers claimed Paganini had such a spooky talent that he could make his violin burst into flames. It was BS, but it filled the concert halls. He never claimed it himself, but he didn't try to stop people from believing it, either." Vicar had heard that story before sometime in the past. "If I had an advantage like that, I would most definitely use it."

"What, and bless lottery tickets for a living? I won't scam people. That would be … disgusting."

"No, not at all. No scam. That would ruin everything, make it cheap. And it would never last. But I would consider just giving everyone an opportunity to meet you, lay eyes on you. Maybe shake your hand. The power of suggestion is strong."

Vicar had watched this very phenomenon in action, aware that it was occurring, yet not quite believing his eyes. He hadn't had to lie about anything. In fact, he hadn't even needed to speak. Everyone else had covered that nicely.

"Other than feeling a little happier now, I really haven't changed one bit." Vicar shrugged.

"With respect, I doubt that. There is no effect without some cause."

Vicar twisted his head and looked off into the distance for a beat. He had indeed been through massive personal changes and had failed to credit them at all. He was Explosive Diarrhea Wedding Elvis no more. He had been so observant of the world around him, yet blind to himself.

Gary continued like the smoothest salesman. "Some folks measure success through purchasing power, how many toys they own. But at a certain point, just buying stuff doesn't work anymore. They give up, maybe get a divorce, and hire lawyers to fight over all the stuff they bought. Then they die, and it was all for nothing."

This line of talk made Vicar prick up his ears. It sounded right.

Gary leaned on the corner of a wire display rack and casually crossed one snakeskin boot in front of the other. "Sometimes folks need someone else to put it all into context for them. Someone to help them gain perspective. They spend so much time worrying about affording *stuff* that any sense of wonder they have is left immature, stunted. They really don't spend a minute developing wonder as a mental tool. Wonder can cause explosions of inspiration, or subtle nuances of the spirit."

Yes, thought Vicar. *This guy understands. Awfully heavy for a friendly chat in a booze shop, but illuminating just the same.* On reflection, Vicar knew that, for all his failings, he had never intentionally overlooked the whimsical, the kooky, or the theme that threaded through.

"These folks are drawn to someone who represents fully formed wonder," Gary continued. "They want to be in that presence or get into that circle because they hope they can just fix everything by contact or osmosis — sort of make up for their lack."

Vicar was feeling strongly persuaded by this man's words. Where the heck had he stumbled in from?

Gary grabbed a bottle of expensive gin and looked it over. "They'll move heaven and earth to make that kind of connection, Tony. They'll usually find it's a disappointment, a cheap facade, no meat on the bones. But occasionally, they are right to make the effort. You don't have to be Nelson Mandela to make a difference. Sometimes the little old lady down the road changes lives, too."

Vicar jolted; did this guy mean Frankie? How could Gary know about his connection to her? He thought of her and how his own neighbourly concern had given rise to her final act of generosity, which she bestowed upon him, thus changing and rerouting his entire path forward. There was no doubt that Frankie had wanted greater good to come of her gesture. She had been, it seemed, a woman with a plan.

Gary looked up at Vicar, underscoring the underlying point with his eyes. He was suggesting that Vicar could make a difference just by being himself. Vicar was not so sure.

"In your case," Gary concluded, "all you're doing is saying hello, nothing further promised or implied. They might come from far away to meet you, and if they do, it'll be darn thoughtful of you to have a hotel room available for the night and a cold pint of beer. Don't you think?"

With Vicar's help, he selected one bottle of very expensive wine and then departed, shaking Vicar's hand as he left.

"Remember, sometimes it only takes an ounce to swing a scale the other direction. Take good care, Tony."

"Thanks. See you around."

Vicar gazed at the Scotches on the far wall, lost in thought for a moment or two, before turning to get another look at the departing man. But the parking lot was completely empty. He squinted in confusion for a second, then shrugged it off.

It occurred to him that he should restock the bottle of expensive wine. Poutine never left too many of them on the shelf, because then they wouldn't seem so rare. But as Vicar passed the rack, he stopped dead. Nothing was missing from the shelf; it was still fully loaded. The bottle of expensive wine had not moved. But Gary had just bought the sole bottle on display — of that, Vicar was sure. He'd handed the bottle over himself. When he went to the computer, he could find no evidence of the transaction that had happened only two minutes ago. It was not listed there. There had to be some mistake. He ran the whole thing through in his mind, concerned that he was starting to lose his marbles.

And then it clicked. He did know the guy, in a way. He recognized that face, all right. Gary had been Julie Northrop's boyfriend, the driver at the accident scene whose life Vicar couldn't save. Had he just received advice from a dead man?

Serena lay in her hospital bed, wigless for a change. Her spiky hair was sticking up in an unkempt mess. The room was guarded by a large, paunchy man with a serious look on his face and a flashlight on his belt the size of a baseball bat.

Wracked with pain and drugged, but insistent, Serena had been requesting "the Vicar" again and again. He did not come.

Her confederates were in various states of disrepair. She'd been told Jeet was hanging on for dear life. At the moment, she couldn't decide if she was still mad, or if she forgave him for attempting to kill her. He had always been the one with the most doubt. Probably the smartest. But not smart enough. Somehow, she knew that Vicar would have wanted her to forgive.

Her shoulder was patched up and tender. A tube led from her arm to an IV tree, and she was connected to a monitor that would beep if she showed signs of deterioration. Her other arm was handcuffed to the bed frame. Lying there floating in misery and confusion, she knew one thing for certain: Vicar was the first man she had ever met who made her consider the possibility that not everyone in the world was out for himself. He was the first man who hadn't tried to wrench her power away. Maybe life didn't always have to be combat, dominance, or submission. Maybe some people cared about more than gaining an advantage. Maybe, just maybe, a man would give up everything for the woman he loved. And maybe some people just *glowed* a little bit.

Serena had felt a kind of spirit within him. He was not cold and reptilian. He was something completely different. How to put it? *Human*. Not fake. Safe. What *was* the right word? He had been willing to swap his life for Jacquie's, and as badly as Serena had wanted him, the gesture had been hard to ignore. Maybe a bit of that love was meant for her, too. And, as hard as it was to swallow, maybe some people were simply *good*.

The nurse gave her another shot. It made the pain abate, but Serena knew it wasn't the medicine she truly needed. She closed her eyes and tried to sleep.

■ ■ ■

At Liquor, having called her over for an impromptu meeting, Vicar said to Jacquie, "You would never believe me if I told you. I just know we hafta do it. We must find a way. I'm certain of it now." The tone in his voice was determined and completely serious.

Jacquie was torn. She could tell that he wasn't fooling around, but she couldn't imagine what new and abstruse artistic vision had propelled his very sudden total commitment.

"What happened, then? A bolt from the blue?"

"If I said that it *was* something like that, would you think I'd fallen out of my tree?"

"You fell out of your tree years ago."

"Right then," he said, ignoring her dig, "let's just call it a *hunch*, then."

Miss C. Jacqueline O'Neil of Tyee Lagoon, British Columbia, never would have thought she'd consent to the biggest deal of her life based on an eccentric's hunch, but after an hour's worth of quibbling with Vicar, she finally ceased her resistance. She realized that, even if it was a swing and a miss, they could still sell the hotel. It was an inheritance, after all. And for heaven's sake, it was legally his. He was clearly suggesting that it was *theirs*. She realized what that meant.

— — —

After two weeks of wandering around in a funk of inexplicable irascibility, Poutine, in a move that surprised even himself, volunteered to move Liquor onto the site of the old coffee shop, forsaking the location that had been his home for over twenty years. The new site was more than large enough, and there was space for warehousing, too. The three of them agreed that they would gut it and make it the new, improved Liquor, hard by the pub, under what they hoped would eventually become a boutique hotel.

Poutine was knee deep in emotions about this move. To Vicar and Jacquie, it was a financial lifeline to an embryonic start-up. To Poutine, it was quite literally an act of faith in his adopted family. He had already realized that these *kids*, as he thought of them, were the nearest thing to kin he had.

Running a business was hard. Running it with your wife — and he dearly hoped Vicar would be smart enough to marry Jacquie someday — was probably even tougher. She was *une belle fille*, as they would have said in Montreal. Poutine considered himself a buffer, there to absorb any of the yuck that might come down the pike in the future. He would never marry himself, of that he felt certain, not unless a gal came around who liked Chevys and Vanna White. But he could maybe be close enough to get a little taste of what it might have been like. He had never planned for a big move like this, but then again, he had never planned to be a bachelor nearing sixty, either. Now that the opportunity presented itself to become part of this great undertaking, he jumped at it. For a man who'd spent his whole life taking pride in his independence, being part of this group felt a little claustrophobic at times but cozy all the same. Plus, they had Twinkies.

■ ■ ■

Farley sat alone in a booth at the pancake house and peered again at the dog-eared newspaper account of the hostage incident, which he kept folded up in the pocket of his jacket, a burgundy blazer made of a flammable fabric, with smile pockets and grime-stained piping. He reread for perhaps the twentieth time the paragraph in which he was mentioned as the quiet hero of the whole thing. One of the papers had printed a photo of him playing bass guitar onstage in his best toque, and referred to him as a "Real Life El Kabong." He liked that. He knew it was silly, but how could anyone take you seriously if you couldn't laugh at yourself? It was a damn sight better than *Connor Rea*. He liked it a lot.

— — —

The hotel's name was deeply entrenched; it had been named the Agincourt for seventy-five years. And yet, Vicar knew it had to be changed. Hardly anyone could even pronounce it correctly, and even fewer knew what it referred to. Knowledge of the Battle of Agincourt had vanished into the mists of history, and Saint Crispin's Day had surely been forgotten even before that. It seemed ironic that the process of opening a pub, which was all about continuity and old-fashioned comfort, would involve renaming the building that contained it. By nature, Vicar was reluctant to mess with something so well established in the community, but he realized that the clientele he would be seeking were far, far away — possibly from distant parts of the world. But for the mysterious legend drawing their attention, they would never otherwise make their way to Tyee Lagoon. At any rate, change never went over well here. Half the residents had probably complained when electricity was first introduced.

Vicar would find a good hotel name eventually. But that was a worry for later. Right now, he had to think about the old beer parlour that was going to become their pub.

Without a good solid name, their planning was missing a major component. The name of a pub gave you the theme, the theme gave you the vibe, and the vibe gave you the pleasure. Several weeks of riffing had amounted to nothing so far. Vicar had proposed every imaginable celebrity and historical figure, from Socrates to Kelly Ripa. None had the right ring. Jacquie, meanwhile, was mired in allegorical names that made Vicar wince: Owl and Pussycat, Daphnis and Chloe, Camelot, Lady of the Lake. At one point, Vicar asked, annoyed, "You've actually been in a pub, right?"

"Of course. Many times."

"How in the hell do your suggestions conjure images of … uhh, lusty good humour and the joy of drinking?"

"I thought you wanted a *nice* name."

"I definitely do, and none of those are. They're more like names for shops in Victoria that sell Tarot cards."

He quickly regretted his crankiness, but his frustration was palpable. They'd been at this for weeks, and some of the paperwork was stalled now, awaiting an official moniker for this grand adventure.

Poutine was getting tired of the constant squabbling, too. "Jesus Christ! Just call it what is: Pub."

Vicar looked dejectedly at Jacquie, then up at the weather-beaten sign outside that read *Liquor*. He sadly shook his head.

"It needs a little more élan than that, Ross."

There was a pause and then all three of them said, in unison, "… Who the hell is Alan?"

— — —

Vicar wandered Tyee Lagoon's tiny downtown, circling the old Agincourt and peering in its front windows, staring off at the trees and looking up at the clouds, racking his mind for a pub name that would hit the nail on the head. He kicked pebbles aimlessly, touched random things like light posts and peeling window frames just to feel their texture. He fingered the registration papers stuffed in his pocket. He was acting like a quirky, wandering crackpot and would have made residents a bit uncomfortable, had they not recognized their famous "vicar" and given him a mulligan.

At the little park on the edge of downtown, he sat down on a bench and watched the squirrels scampering around and felt his tires spinning. A lady with a little dog in a stupid cardigan — his elementary school science teacher, in fact — passed him, looking on with some disapproval as he chatted to himself just a little too loudly. She steered over to the edge of the sidewalk and glared.

Realizing that his behaviour was annoying the elderly and possibly freaking out small children, Vicar got up. He was at the end of his patience, anyway. He marched the long road back to Liquor.

When he arrived, he plopped down on a stool at the side counter. Jacquie had already arrived and was waiting there for him. He handed the registration papers to her.

"That's it. I am totally stumped." He looked heavenward. "I'm clearly not going to get it. So you do it, Jacquie. Whatever you write down is the name we're going with."

She looked at him doubtfully. "Anything I write? No matter what?"

"Well, don't write something like *This Place Sucks*. But any reasonable name for a pub I will accept."

Jacquie grinned mischievously. She chewed the end of the pen for a few moments, thinking through the last few months of chaos and fascinating madness, then she confidently wrote something down. She folded the application form in her hand and said, "There."

"Just like that, huh?"

"Yup."

"What does it say?"

"Not tellin'. I'm mailing it in, and you'll find out in a couple of weeks."

■ ■ ■

Fifteen days later, a letter arrived in Vicar's mailbox addressed to

> The Vicar's Knickers Public House
> c/o Anthony Vicar
> P.O. Box 101
> Tyee Lagoon, British Columbia V0R 9P9

And so it began.

Acknowledgements

Thanks to Pete McCormack, the funniest polymath on Earth, who has encouraged me for decades and is, among many other high-achieving things, a brilliant author. Also, thank you to Cindy Labonte-Smith, my lost and then found-again elementary-school chum, author, teacher, and aviatrix, who chucked ideas at me like requests at a karaoke bar and advised brilliantly at the earliest stages. Barry Munn, author, translator of eleventeen languages, and retired MD, who unstintingly read, commented, encouraged, and introduced me to the saltiest breakfast in creation, kippers. Patricia Stirling, who read and then reread ... *and then re-reread*, all while lounging on the hood of a car in a parking lot, sipping Vino Verde. Vancouver's sexiest historian, Aaron Chapman, took innumerable calls from an aimless neophyte and always had a good suggestion and a kind word of encouragement. Scott Steedman set me on the correct path. Duke Thornley pulled and J.J. Martin pushed me through the door. Thanks to Cpl. Tammy Douglas of the RCMP for advice on hostage situations, and Chris Churchill, Esq. for discussions about Canadian law. Jenny McWha oversaw completion and delivery of my splat of alphabet soup. Catharine Chen must have felt she was hand-ironing the bumps out of a highway. Shannon Whibbs, prickly only when provoked, led this giant horse through the hospital of sub edits.

Much love to my Spirit of the West family, living and dead, young and old, every single one of them. They go nameless because they number in the dozens. Darren "Smitty" Smith: thanks for the organ, in case I forgot to mention it before. Ian Bryce — sorry about cocking up your tractor that time. Denis Collins, for correct Irish spellings and pronunciations; Peter Winn, for his secret wine cellar — don't even bother looking, it's hidden like the lost city of El Dorado. Mark Vinden possesses the rare good grace to doze off when I flirt with Suzie. Also, a reverential bow to Melanie Martin, Baroness of the Magical Duchies of Dildo and Come By Chance, NFLD. Kevin Herbert Peterson and family — ugh!

Perry, Sam, and Amy, as well as our large extended family, must be strongly advised that any resemblance to persons living or dead is purely coincidental. I am nearly serious. Ha ha to the fitness app on my phone that has no idea at least one kilometre of my daily "steps" come from wandering to the coffee pot. Speaking of fitness, I thank Kiyomi and Naomi, the

"Renal Twins" — *they'll be appearing all week in the lounge* ... And, most especially, to my long-suffering wife, Merm, who is delighted I've gotten this book to press but still doesn't understand how a man can believe it's reasonable to spend so much time in pyjamas, gesticulating and mumbling.

RIP: Johnny & Maestro George.

About the Author

Lifelong musician and member of Vancouver musical group Spirit of the West since dinosaurs roamed the earth, Vince Ditrich began writing on college ruled paper with a Bic pen in the previous century and has never really ceased since. He has written for numerous publications through the years; has his own e-magazine, *Random Note Generator*; and is currently negotiating a huge financial deal, via email, with a Nigerian prince who needs help with a wire transfer of $100,000,000.00. Since moving to the west coast from an undisclosed location in the 1980s, Vince has earned almost a dozen gold and platinum albums, enshrinement in various Halls of Fame, and, along with his beloved bandmates, a lovely star in the sidewalk on Vancouver's Starwalk, which is at this point probably covered in old gum and pee. He lives on Vancouver Island.

TONY VICAR WILL BE
BACK FOR ANOTHER
MILDLY CATASTROPHIC
MISADVENTURE IN

THE VICAR'S KNICKERS

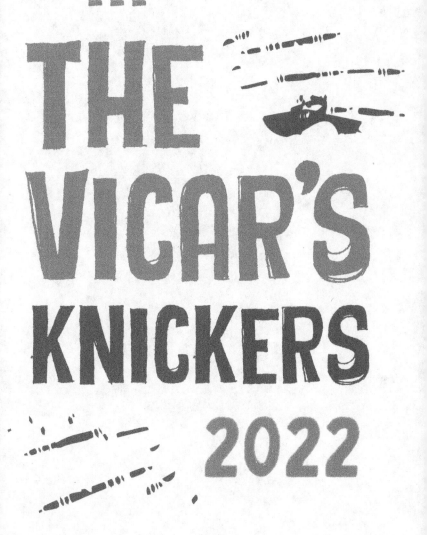

2022